For Ellen Krieger

JOIN THE FUN
IN CABIN SIX . . .

KATIE is the perfect team player. She loves competitive games, planned activities, and coming up with her own great ideas.

MEGAN would rather lose herself in fantasyland than get into organized fun.

SARAH would be much happier if she could spend her time reading instead of exerting herself.

ERIN is much more interested in boys, clothes, and makeup than in playing kids' games at camp.

TRINA hates conflicts. She just wants everyone to be happy . . .

AND THEY ARE! Despite all their differences, the Cabin Six bunch are having the time of their lives at CAMP SUNNYSIDE!

Look for More Fun and Games with
CAMP SUNNYSIDE FRIENDS
by Marilyn Kaye
from Avon Camelot

MARILYN KAYE is the author of many popular books for young readers, including the "Out of This World" series and the "Sisters" books. She is an associate professor at St. John's University and lives in Brooklyn, New York.

Camp Sunnyside is the camp Marilyn Kaye wishes that she had gone to every summer when she was a kid.

Avon Books are available at special quantity discounts for bulk purchases for sales promotions, premiums, fund raising or educational use. Special books, or book excerpts, can also be created to fit specific needs.

For details write or telephone the office of the Director of Special Markets, Avon Books, Dept. FP, 105 Madison Avenue, New York, New York 10016, 212-481-5653.

Erin and the Movie Star

Marilyn Kaye

AN AVON CAMELOT BOOK

CAMP SUNNYSIDE FRIENDS #10: ERIN AND THE MOVIE STAR is an original publication of Avon Books. This work has never before appeared in book form.

AVON BOOKS
A division of
The Hearst Corporation
105 Madison Avenue
New York, New York 10016

First Avon Camelot Printing: February 1991

CAMELOT TRADEMARK REG. U.S. PAT. OFF. AND IN OTHER COUNTRIES, MARCA REGISTRADA, HECHO EN U.S.A.

Printed in the U.S.A.

OPM 10 9 8 7 6 5 4 3 2 1

Chapter 1

A stream of sunshine hit Erin's pillow, and her eyes opened. For one wonderful second, she thought she was at home, snuggled under the frilly peach comforter on her canopy bed. Then she saw the plain white sheets and the simple cotton blanket stamped with that tacky sunshine logo. Camp Sunnyside was nothing like home, that was for sure.

Glancing around, Erin sighed wearily. She'd been at camp for almost two months, but it felt like forever. Coming back to the place where she'd spent every summer since she was eight had been her parents' idea, not hers. Erin would much rather have been at home, hanging out with her friends and checking out boys at the country club or the mall.

Oh, it wasn't that Camp Sunnyside was a terrible place to be or anything like that. Not if you were a kid. When she was younger, she'd had some great times with the other girls in cabin six. But things had changed. Erin had grown up, and they hadn't. They were still eleven years old, and she was already twelve. With makeup, she could pass for fourteen.

And it didn't help that her eleven-year-old bunkmates had been acting like babies all week. Like they were doing right this minute.

"I mean it, Sarah," Katie yelled from her top bunk bed. "I couldn't sleep all night because of that stupid flashlight! Can't you get your reading done during the day?"

Sarah, sitting on the opposite top bunk, glared at Katie from behind her glasses. She pulled her knees up under her chin and said, "How can you even see the flashlight? It's under my blanket, and your bed is all the way on the other side of the room."

"It makes funny shadows on the ceiling," Katie insisted. "They keep me awake."

"It didn't bother you at the beginning of the summer," Sarah pointed out.

"Well, it bothers me now," Katie stated.

Erin watched Katie climb down from her bed. Katie was the kind of person who just *had* to get the last word in.

"It's just a flashlight," Katie's best friend Trina said, to no one in particular and all of them in general. Trina was like that—always trying to smooth things out, always trying to

2

reason with people. As Katie climbed down past her, Trina shot her a pleading look, as if to say, "let's not have any more fights."

Erin could agree with that. There had been an unusual amount of cabin bickering this past week. "*Good* morning, everybody!" Erin sang out. But her voice dripped with sarcasm. The other girls weren't hiding *their* Camp Sunnyside slumps very well, so why should she?

She slipped out of bed—the only single bed in the cabin—and leaned over the little table next to it. Opening up the top drawer, Erin looked at her blue satin makeup bag. Today probably wasn't worth using up her new eyeliner sticks, she decided. After all, there were no boys at Camp Sunnyside. So what was the sense in looking good?

"Megan, I was surprised you didn't get a demerit yesterday for your bed," Trina told the tiny redhead, who had just bounded out of her bed and over to her bureau.

A toothbrush in one hand, open toothpaste tube in the other, Megan squinted at the rumpled sheets. "What was wrong with it?" she asked.

Trina eyed her reprovingly. "What's wrong with it was, you didn't even make it."

"I did, too!" Megan insisted hotly.

"It was all lumpy. And you never tuck your sheets in properly." Trina sounded really an-

3

noyed, Erin noticed. Super-tidy Trina couldn't stand for anything, or anybody, to be messy.

"The problem is that you make yours too neat," Megan declared. "That's what makes mine look sloppy."

"Nice try, Megan," Erin said dryly as she took out a fresh Camp Sunnyside tee shirt. Today, she was going to try tying the bottom of it at the waist like the older girls in cabin nine. And even if she wasn't going to wear eye makeup, she was definitely going to put on some lipstick. She had to keep up her image, even if it was just for her own cabin mates.

Suddenly, Katie let out a sound that was somewhere between a moan and a scream. That got everyone's attention.

"What's the matter?" Trina asked.

Katie held up an open copy of *Teen Scene* magazine. "Check out this picture of Rod Laney. Isn't it incredible? He's so gorgeous."

"Of course he's gorgeous," Sarah said. "He's a movie star. But since when did you go boy-crazy?"

"Rod Laney isn't a boy," Katie said with dignity. "He's a man. If boys looked like this, maybe I wouldn't mind having them around."

"Hey, that's my magazine!" Megan declared. "I've been looking all over for it. You shouldn't have taken it without asking."

There they go again, Erin thought as she

4

pulled a brush through her silky blonde hair. Bickering with one another over something stupid, like a movie star. It seemed to be a part of every summer—there would come a week when nothing went smoothly, and everybody fought over everything. Swearing that this would be her last year at Sunnyside, no matter what, Erin decided to go see if the mail had come in yet. Mail was like a lifeline for her!

She quickly finished dressing. Running out the door with a quick "see you," Erin hurried across the lawn to the reception area where the mailboxes were located.

A happy smile crossed her face the second she saw her compartment. Erin lifted out two pieces of mail. One was a postcard from her mom and dad in Cannes, France. And the other—even better—was a letter! Erin recognized her friend Marcia's bold, backslanting handwriting on the envelope.

She scanned the postcard as she stepped outside and parked herself under a tree near the dining hall. Her parents wrote that they were fine. The beaches were lovely, the weather was delightful, blah, blah, blah. . . . They hoped Erin was having her "traditional" fun at Camp Sunnyside, and they'd see her soon.

Rolling her eyes and stuffing the postcard in her back pocket, Erin eagerly ripped open the

5

fat pink envelope. Leaning against the tree, she began to read:

Dear Erin,

How are things going for you at Camp Prisonside? Did they put an electric fence around the place to keep you there? Ha-ha. Just kidding.

So far, summer has been fabulous! I got back from Paris in June. It was awesome, and you won't believe the new clothes I got there. My parents just gave me a credit card and said, "have a good time!" Wait till you see . . .

Erin's smile melted a little. Not too long ago, Marcia, who had always been a skinny kid, had developed a dynamite figure. She really knew how to dress it, too. Even though Marcia was just about her best friend back home, Erin still hoped she wouldn't look *too* good in the fall— not better than *her*, at least.

Anyway, after I got back, I settled into a routine of lotsa beach, pool, sand, sun, and checking out lots of YOU KNOW WHATS. (Boys! Aaaaaaa!!!) You should see some of the guys hanging around the country club pool, Erin. I mean, they are gorgeous, capital G, plus! Did you know that Jenny Lennard has an older brother? He's fifteen. I guess we

6

never met him because he goes to prep school. He's got these incredible green eyes and eyelashes that go on forever.

Erin had to smile. Marcia was like a Geiger counter when it came to boys. If there was a cute guy within ten miles, Marcia would be sure to find him. Unless Erin found him first.

Oh! Listen to this! Remember how Jessica Meyers had those pictures taken, and she was acting real secretive about them? Well, it turns out she was applying to the Miss Junior Miss contest—and guess what!—she got in! Isn't that unbelievable? I think you're so much prettier than her, too. She gets to go to New York in the fall and everything!

Erin's jaw dropped about a foot. Jessica Meyers! A Miss Junior Miss contestant! Why, Jessica had been wearing braces just a couple of months ago! Now she'd be the star of the new school year. The whole town would be buzzing about her.

A wave of jealousy washed over Erin. Why hadn't *she* applied for the Miss Junior Miss contest? She'd seen the poster in the school cafeteria like everybody else, but there had been so many rules and regulations about entering that it hadn't seemed worth it. What a mistake. Now, she'd have to live through months and months of Jessica Meyers flaunting her newfound fame in everyone's face!

I really miss you! Hope you get out early. Do they parole people for good behavior? If so, I'm sure you'll be in camp for a long time! Ha-ha!

Oh, by the way, I hate to mention this, but I saw a certain boy with the initials A.R. at the mall—and he was holding hands with a girl!

That's right—it was Alan!

Boy, Erin, what a rat he is! He has no loyalty to you at all. The girl was real cute, too. He got all red when he saw me coming, and he even dropped Mystery Girl's hand. By the way, just so you know who your *real* friends are, I didn't even say "hi" to him. I just gave him a dirty look and kept walking. What a creep! I mean, how could he do something like that to you?

Erin slumped against the tree and let out a humongous groan. She felt like she'd just been punched in the stomach. Her boyfriend, Alan, holding hands with a girl at the mall. How could he? Of course, she and Alan had never made any promises to each other. And she herself had a little flirtation going with a boy at Camp Ea-

8

gle across the lake. But still! Alan hadn't even written to her all summer. On the other hand, she hadn't written him, either.

Erin's eyes moved down to the bottom of Marcia's letter. The rest was just hugs and kisses. With lips set tightly, Erin folded the pink paper and fit it back inside the envelope. She was totally furious. How could Alan do that to her? Everyone knew they'd sort of been going together. And even though she couldn't say she was madly in love with him, everyone would know he had dumped her. Gritting her teeth in rage, she thought, he'll be sorry, that creep. Stuffing the mail in her pocket, she headed back toward the cabin.

"Hurry! It's pancake day!" she heard Katie shout as she and the other girls raced out of cabin six and headed for the dining hall. Their counselor, Carolyn, was with them. Now the others were whooping it up like little kids, yelling "Pancakes! Pancakes!" all over the quad.

Trina must have seen something in Erin's expression. "What's the matter? Did you get some bad news or something?" she asked, searching Erin's face with her steady brown eyes.

If only Erin could tell Trina what the problem really was—her whole world was crumbling. Her friends were having a super summer in Europe, at the pool, shopping their heads off, and getting picked to be Miss Junior Miss contestants. Her

9

boyfriend had been seen holding hands with another girl, and here she was, stuck at Camp Rinkydink.

"Nothing's wrong. I'm fine." There was no way Trina would understand. None of them would. They'd never even had a boyfriend, and they certainly didn't have friends who went to Paris or got picked for the Miss Junior Miss Contest.

"Come on then, Erin," Trina said, still looking concerned. "They're having pancakes."

Pancakes. Big deal.

"Whoopee. Okay. I'm coming," Erin answered.

In the dining hall, Erin took her place on line behind Megan. The other girls were oohing and aahing about the blueberry syrup, but Erin just took her plate and went to sit next to Sarah, who had already wolfed down practically an entire plate of pancakes.

"Girls! I have an announcement!" Ms. Winkle rapped on the edge of a table with a spoon to get all the campers' attention. Erin noticed that the camp director looked more flustered than usual. "This week, we're going to be having some guests at Camp Sunnyside."

A murmur went up from the campers at the tables. The cabin six girls all looked at one another expectantly. The last time Ms. Winkle had said that, a swarm of boys from nearby Camp

Eagle had descended on Sunnyside. For Erin, it had been sheer heaven!

Ms. Winkle held up a hand for silence. "I see you're all curious, so I won't keep you in suspense. It's a film crew. They're going to be shooting a movie here at Camp Sunnyside."

An excited buzz started going around the room as soon as the word "movie" came out of Ms. Winkle's mouth. Erin felt a tingle shoot up and down her spine. A film crew—here at Sunnyside!

"What's the movie going to be about?" someone asked.

"I'm not sure, actually," Ms. Winkle answered. "Something about a summer camp, I suppose. All you need to know is that they're going to be using our facilities to shoot some scenes. And they're going to need the cooperation of every one of us."

"You mean, they need our help?" an excited voice called out.

Ms. Winkle shook her head. "Goodness, no. The crew is simply using our camp for some of their 'locations.' Our job will be staying out of their way."

Over the chorus of disappointed groans, Ms. Winkle had to raise her voice. "But some of the crew may be eating in our dining hall, and you may even see some of the actors around the camp. I'd like you to treat them with our traditional Camp Sunnyside politeness. But please don't bother them or ask them any questions about the movie. We'll be sure to hear about it in time, and we can all go see it when it comes out next summer. Right now, the film people have to be left alone so they can do their work. Does everyone understand?"

A chorus of reluctant yesses went up from the campers. Ms. Winkle thanked them, then went back to her table.

"Wow," Erin said, her heart beating so loudly she was afraid the whole room could hear it.

"I wonder who's in it," Katie said, her eyes bright with excitement. "I mean, there must be a star in it."

As her bunkmates debated the possibilities of who might be in the movie, Erin's mind was elsewhere. A secret plan was beginning to brew in her head.

What if she, Erin Chapman, managed to get a part in a real feature film? That would make this whole miserable summer at Camp Sunnyside worth it. Being in a movie was even better than being a Miss Junior Miss contestant—and it was miles better than a trip to Europe and a bunch of foreign clothes!

So what if Ms. Winkle had said that none of the campers would be involved? How could she be so sure? After all, new movie stars were discovered in all sorts of places, weren't they?

12

Drugstores, street corners—why not a summer camp?

The scene played out in her mind. She'd be strolling across the campgrounds. An important-looking man would stop her. "Excuse me. Are you an actress?"

"Not exactly."

"Well, you should be! You'd be perfect in this film."

Once the movie people saw her, Erin reflected, *of course* they would put her in the film! She was beautiful, everyone knew that. And it just so happened that she was talented as well. Hadn't she blown everybody away earlier in the summer when she played the part of the Spirit of Happiness in the Sunnyside Spectacular? After her performance, everyone had complimented her about how great an actress she was.

Erin pushed her portion of half-eaten pancakes away. Her thoughts were racing. This was so perfect! She could just imagine the looks on Marcia's and Jessica's faces when she told them she had a part in a real film. Marcia would pretend to be so happy, but inside, she'd be dying of envy. And Jessica would be absolutely crushed! Erin would have to treat them all very graciously, just to help them get over their jealousy.

But there was one person she wouldn't be so nice to. Not at first anyway. Not unless he got down on his knees and begged her for forgiveness. *Alan.*

Mystery Girl—ha! Was he ever going to regret betraying Erin while she was locked away at Camp Prisonside.

Chapter 2

"Girls, after breakfast, I've got a meeting in Ms. Winkle's office." Carolyn wiped her mouth with a napkin, and looked over at the girls of cabin six. "Think you can go back to the cabin and straighten up by yourselves?"

Erin rolled her eyes. Why did Carolyn always have to treat them like such infants?

"Sure, Carolyn," Trina answered.

"But do a good job, okay? I really want the place to look great." Carolyn's eyes panned around the table, stopping for a second when they got to Megan. As usual, Megan was staring off into space, looking like she'd left planet Earth completely. "Megan?" Carolyn said, snapping her fingers.

"Huh?" said Megan, coming out of it.

"We'll do a super cleanup, you'll see," Trina promised, coming to the rescue. "Right, Megan?" Megan nodded her agreement, and Carolyn went off to her meeting.

"I'm all finished," Katie announced, pushing her empty plate away and drinking up her orange juice. "Come on, everybody!"

Erin stood up with the rest of the girls and followed Katie out of the dining hall. The minute they got outside, she glanced around to make sure no one else was listening. "Listen," she told them. "I've got something to do. I'll see you guys later."

"What?" Trina's eyes widened with curiosity. "Where are you going, Erin? We're supposed to clean up. Didn't you hear what Carolyn said?"

Erin brushed that aside. "I've got to go somewhere, okay? Can't a person have any privacy around here?"

Katie narrowed her eyes and aimed them straight at Erin's. "Something's going on in that devious little mind of yours. Tell us what."

Leave it to Katie to be so suspicious. Erin bit her lip and considered. She hated to let them in on something like this, but on the other hand, if she told them her plan, they could cover for her if she needed it. "I'm going to spy on Ms. Winkle's meeting so I can find out about the movie."

Katie's face broke into an immediate grin. But Trina looked alarmed. "We're not supposed

16

to go around spying! You're going to get into trouble, Erin."

"Come on, Trina," Erin said, "It won't actually be spying. Just . . . *listening,* that's all."

Katie looked amazed. "Trina, don't you want to know about the movie?"

"Sure I do," Trina said hesitantly. "But Carolyn said we were supposed to—"

"Forget Carolyn," Erin said, getting annoyed. "I'm going to find out everything, and then I'll tell all of you. If I'm not back at the cabin when Carolyn comes for inspection, just say—um, that I got a phone call."

Trina looked dubious, but Katie seemed to go for the idea. "Maybe I should go with you," she said.

Erin shook her head. "No, it's safer if I go alone. In case I get caught or something."

"Come on," Sarah said. "We better get back to the cabin." She and Megan started walking away.

Trina shifted from one foot to the other, looking worried. "I don't think this is a very good idea."

"I think it's an excellent idea!" Katie told her.

"Well, who's going to tell Carolyn why Erin isn't there? Not me!" Trina insisted. "I'm not going to lie!"

"I'll tell her," Katie offered. "I'll just cross my fingers behind my back when I do."

How incredibly childish! Erin let out a sigh, and began walking back down the pathway. "See you guys later."

"Good luck!" Katie called out, more loudly than she should have.

Erin stepped gingerly off the path and started sneaking behind the row of bushes that led down to the staff quarters.

What luck! Ms. Winkle's window was wide open. Erin crouched down and sneaked under it. Inside, she could hear the camp director talking.

"Naturally," Ms. Winkle was saying, "the girls are going to be curious. I don't want our regular camp activities disrupted because of the filming, but at the same time, we don't want to disturb the film people. You'll all be getting copies of the shooting schedule each day so that you can work around the filming and keep the campers away."

Erin heard Carolyn's voice. "Are you going to tell them who's in the movie?"

"Hmm . . ." Ms. Winkle sounded unsure. "I'd like to tell them, but I don't want to cause any commotion. If the girls find out Rod Laney is at Camp Sunnyside, there could be a riot."

Rod Laney! Wait till Katie heard *that.*

"I have an idea!" came another voice floating out of the window. It sounded like Donna, the arts and crafts counselor. "Maybe we could tell the girls he's going to be here, and then

18

ask him to speak to the girls. That way the campers would get to see Rod Laney in person, and they'd also learn a little bit about how a film is made."

"That's a good idea, Donna," Ms. Winkle replied. "Unfortunately, the director has already told me that he and the others are working on a terribly tight schedule. Based on what he said, I just don't think they'll have time for something like that."

"How are they going to handle casting the extras, Ms. Winkle?" This question came from Darrell, Sunnyside's super-gorgeous swimming instructor. "I know you didn't want the girls to know about it beforehand, but don't the movie people have to get a look at the campers to decide which girls are going to be in the film?"

Erin stifled a gasp of surprise. The movie people were going to be using campers as extras! This was the best news Erin had heard yet—getting discovered might be even easier than she thought.

"Ah, yes, the extras," Ms. Winkle said. "That's something else we're going to have to discuss. The casting director has given me a preliminary list of just how many girls they'll need and—oh dear!" Ms. Winkle let out a sudden gasp. "My papers! They're blowing all over!"

"I'll shut the window," Darrell said, his voice getting closer.

19

That was Erin's exit line. On tiptoe, she hurried away, praying that no one would see her. But she couldn't keep from smiling. Suddenly, Camp Sunnyside wasn't such a bad place after all. The minute she got back onto the path, she broke into a run.

Katie must have seen her coming, because the cabin door flew open the minute Erin got to it. "So? What'd you find out?" Katie demanded to know, pulling her inside.

"Hang on, let me catch my breath," Erin told her, flopping down on her bed.

"Well?" Megan prodded. "Well? Did you learn anything?"

Even Trina stopped wiping the top of her bureau and turned to Erin.

Sarah looked up and closed her book, though she kept one finger tucked inside to mark her place. "So?"

Tapping her foot, Katie put her hands on her hips and stared at Erin. "Are you going to tell us? Or are you going to let us die of curiosity?" she demanded.

Erin propped herself up on one elbow. "You don't have to be so anxious," she said casually. "After all, it's only a movie."

"Only a movie? Come on," Megan begged. "Tell us! Who's going to be in it?"

"How long are they going to be here?" Katie asked.

Erin fixed her eyes on the coat of Pink Passion nail polish she was wearing. "Well, let's see . . . now who did I hear was the star? Oh yeah. Rod Laney."

Katie went pale. *"Rod Laney."*

Erin nodded. "He's going to be right here at Camp Sunnyside."

"I'm going to faint," said Katie, leaning on the back of the nearest chair. "Rod Laney. Ohmigosh. I can't believe it. I can't *believe* it!"

"Also, Ms. Winkle was lying this morning. They *are* going to use some of the campers as extras in the film."

"They're going to use campers as extras?" a dumbstruck Megan repeated.

"That's what I said."

"Not me, I hope," Sarah said. "I'd be too nervous."

Erin ran a hand through her silky blonde hair. "I think it would be kind of fun, being an extra. At least it's better than doing some stupid arts and crafts project."

"I wonder if you have to do an audition for something like that?" Katie wondered.

"A what?" Megan asked, cocking her red head to one side.

"An audition, a tryout," Katie said. "You remember, like you did for the Spectacular." She clasped her hands to her chest. "Oh, Romeo, Romeo," she declared dramatically, "wherefore art thou Romeo?"

"Huh?" said Megan, squinting at Katie.

"That's from *Romeo and Juliet.* It's called the balcony speech because Juliet says it on a balcony. A girl at my school used it to audition for our school play."

"I have a copy of *Romeo and Juliet,*" Sarah said. "It's a great play."

"Can I see it?" Erin asked. "If I'm going to audition, I'll need to learn a speech."

"Sure," Sarah said.

Just then the door to the cabin swung open and Carolyn walked in. "Hi, everybody!" the counselor said. "What's going on?"

"We were just finishing our cleanup," Trina said.

Erin quickly reached over to straighten out her bedspread.

"What's that you're reading, Erin?" Carolyn asked.

Erin looked down at the book in her hand as if she had never seen it before. "This? It's just *Romeo and Juliet,* by William Shakespeare."

Carolyn's eyebrows went up. "You're reading Shakespeare? I've never seen you with any reading matter except magazines, Erin. What gives?"

Fortunately, an excuse came to her. "I need to read it for school next semester."

It was pretty lame, but thankfully, Carolyn didn't press her about it. "Well, guys," said the counselor, "except for Megan's bed, this cabin looks fine."

Megan grinned. "I don't see what the big deal is. I'm only going to mess it up again tonight."

Carolyn gave up. "Try to do a better job tomorrow, okay? You'd all better get into your swimsuits. It's almost time for your lesson. And you know Darrell doesn't like you to be late."

"Oooooh, Darrell!" The girls placed their hands on their hearts and swooned in unison, as they always did when Darrell's name was mentioned. For once, even Erin joined in. She was in such a good mood that she didn't mind acting like an idiot just this once.

"I think I'll go to the pool with you guys today," Carolyn said. "I feel like a swim."

"Carolyn, I'm not going to the pool," Erin said, wrinkling her forehead as if she were in pain. "I've got my period. And unbelievable cramps."

Carolyn looked at her curiously. "You seemed fine at breakfast, Erin."

"Well, I've got cramps now, so I'd really like to stay here and lie down for a while." She held her stomach to make Carolyn think she really had cramps.

"Do you want to go to the infirmary?" Carolyn asked.

"No, thanks," Erin said, giving her best imitation of a brave smile. "I'll be okay."

"All right," said Carolyn, turning to the others. "Let's go, girls!"

As they walked out of the cabin, the other girls all shot Erin secret looks. They knew she didn't have cramps, but they didn't know exactly what she was up to.

The minute they were gone, Erin turned back to her bed. She picked up the copy of *Romeo and Juliet* and started searching for the balcony speech Katie had talked about. After all, if she was going to give a great audition, she'd better start rehearsing.

"Romeo, Romeo, wherefore art thou Romeo? Deny they father and refuse thy name . . ."

Erin said the words out loud, enjoying the sound of her voice as she spoke. She'd always suspected she was a born actress.

"Or if thou wilt not, be but sworn my love, and I'll no longer be a Capulet . . ."

What in the world did *that* mean? What was a Capulet, some sort of hat or something? And come to think of it, what kind of a word was "wherefore?" And "wilt?" Why did people use such weird language in the old days, anyway?

Erin closed the book and looked at the cover. In her opinion, William Shakespeare wasn't all he was cracked up to be. Still, if she was going to audition for a part in the film, she'd have to learn the stupid speech.

Greatness demands sacrifice, Erin told herself, opening the book again and getting back to work.

Chapter 3

"Romeo, Romeo, wherefore art thou Romeo?" Erin stood in the middle of the cabin the following morning, reciting the balcony speech while the other girls looked on in amazement. At first Erin felt a little foolish, and a couple of times, she had to look at the book to make sure of what the next line was. But still, she thought, acting was pretty easy. And with her looks, who would care if she forgot a line or two?

"And for thy name, which is no part of thee, take all myself!" When she got to the last line, Erin held her breath a long time and stared out, over the tops of her friends' heads, as if she were too much in love with Romeo to say anything more. Then she broke out in a big smile and bent from the waist in a low bow. She had been fabulous, she could just tell! Straightening up, she waited for a burst of applause.

But Trina, Katie, Sarah, and Megan were

staring at her in disbelief. They were probably so knocked out by her performance that they couldn't think of anything to say.

"So? What did you think?"

Katie turned to Trina, who turned to Megan, who shot a quick look at Sarah. Sarah looked back at Katie, and so did everybody else.

"Well," Katie said, finally. "I think it was just, uh . . . fine."

"Me, too," Trina added quickly, nodding with an enthusiasm that seemed just a little too energetic.

"I thought it was really impressive that you were able to memorize such a long speech," said Sarah.

Then Katie, Trina, Sarah, and Erin turned to Megan, because she was the only girl who hadn't said anything yet.

"What was the speech about?" Megan asked, tilting her head to one side.

"It's about Juliet," Erin answered impatiently. "She loves Romeo, and she wants to go out with him."

Megan nodded slowly, a thoughtful look on her face. "Oh," she said. "I get it." The look on her face said she *didn't* get it. But then, that was Megan. The speech was probably too sophisticated for her.

"I'm hungry," Sarah announced. "Where's Carolyn?"

27

"In her room," said Trina. "Megan, what are you staring at?"

Megan had her face pressed against the window. "There's a bunch of trucks coming up the main road." The others gathered around her and peered down.

"Four Star Productions," Sarah said, reading the name on the side of a huge red and yellow truck.

"That must be the movie crew!" Katie said, pushing through the others to get a look out the window.

Erin shivered with excitement. The movie people were actually here! But she tried to look nonchalant. "Where *is* Carolyn? I'm hungry."

"Here I am," Carolyn said, emerging from her room. "What's up?" She joined them at the window.

The girls watched until the trucks went around a curve and out of sight.

"Those were the movie trucks," Megan told Carolyn.

Carolyn nodded. "Let's go eat." Together, they left the cabin.

"I wonder if Rod Laney was on one of those trucks," Katie said.

Erin shot Katie a fierce look, but it was too late. "How did you know Rod Laney was in the movie?" Carolyn asked.

Katie gulped. "Oh, I heard a rumor. You know there are no secrets at Sunnyside."

Carolyn still looked quizzical, but she let it pass. "I think the stars usually travel by car—maybe even by limousine," she told Katie.

"Oh, Carolyn," Katie sighed, "do you think I'll be able to get Rod Laney's autograph? It would be the greatest thing that ever happened in my entire life!"

"I don't think you should get your hopes up, Katie. Ms. Winkle really doesn't want any of us bothering the movie people. Remember, they're here to work, not play." Carolyn glanced at each girl in turn. The warning was definitely meant for all of them.

"Okay," said a disappointed Katie, as they walked into the dining hall. "I get the message."

"Yuck, scrambled eggs," Megan said, when they saw what was being served for breakfast. "They're really gross."

"I love scrambled eggs," Sarah said. But Erin hardly heard them. Her attention was on the door of the dining hall. Ms. Winkle had just walked in with a man Erin had never seen before.

Hardly paying attention to what food landed on her plate, Erin eyed the man carefully. He was about thirty, Erin guessed, and he had a neatly trimmed light brown beard. And then it

29

hit her. He must be one of the movie people. Probably the director of the film. He had that important look.

"Carolyn, who's that man sitting with Ms. Winkle?" Katie asked as they all took seats at their usual table.

Carolyn shrugged. "I really don't know, Katie."

Erin knew. But just because *she* had figured out who the man was didn't mean she was going to start blabbing it to everybody else.

She had to find a way to get his attention. There were a lot of girls in the dining hall, and somehow, she had to get him to notice *her*.

"I'm going to get another roll," Erin said, pushing her chair away from the table.

Carolyn gave her a strange look. "You already have two," she said, pointing to the uneaten bread on Erin's plate.

"I'm hungry," Erin lied, as she headed toward the front of the room where Ms. Winkle and the movie director sat.

As soon as she got near them, Erin took a deep breath. First impressions were very important. she had to make this one count.

"Excuse me, Ms. Winkle," she said as she approached their table.

"Yes, dear? How can I help you?"

Erin's eyes were aimed at the man sitting next to Ms. Winkle. "Ms. Winkle," she said, with what she hoped was a warm smile. "I don't think I've ever told you this before, but in my opinion, Camp Sunnyside is just the most fantastic place to spend the summer! It's just *so wonderful* here!"

The man looked a little startled, but he seemed to nod in approval. Erin turned back to Ms. Winkle, beaming her best thousand-watt smile.

"Why, thank you, dear," Ms. Winkle said. "It's nice to know our campers are enjoying themselves."

Erin had watched enough actresses on TV talk shows to know what to say next. "Really, Ms. Winkle," she said, glancing at her briefly, then gazing deep into the eyes of the man beside her. "My experience at this camp has been—absolutely—*fabulous.* I just *love* being here, with all my heart. I really, really do."

Ms. Winkle looked at Erin strangely. But Erin was pleased at the man's reaction. He was smiling pleasantly.

"So, you see, well—I just *had* to tell you," Erin said, finishing up. Then, with one last, lingering smile, she walked back to her table. Mission accomplished.

"What was that all about?" Katie wanted to know when Erin took her seat again.

Katie had to be the biggest busybody in the

entire solar system. "I told you," Erin said, a little annoyed. "I just went to get another roll."

"That's funny." Katie looked at Erin's empty hands.

"Oh! I forgot!" Erin realized, jumping up and heading for the food line.

When she got back to the table, Erin dug into her eggs, a satisfied gleam in her eye. The movie director really liked her. She could tell.

The girls ate the rest of their breakfasts without talking much. Megan was saying something about playing tennis, and Sarah talked about a book she was reading. But Erin didn't pay any attention. She kept stealing glances at Ms. Winkle's table. After the camp director and the man she was with finished their food, they sat there for a long time, chatting.

"I have to go talk to the other counselors," Carolyn said, standing up and pushing her chair back under the table. "I'll meet you back in the cabin in ten minutes. Okay?"

"Sure, Carolyn," Trina said, watching her walk away.

"Come on, Erin, aren't you finished yet?" Katie asked. "I want to get inspection over with. We've got free swim today!"

Erin liked free swim days. It was a chance to work on her tan. But today, she was determined to linger at breakfast until she had another chance to make an impression on the movie director.

"You go ahead without me," she said to her cabin mates. "I'll be there in a minute."

"Why?" asked Trina, shooting Erin a puzzled look.

"Um, I need to see someone." She looked around, pretending to be searching the crowd now milling toward the door.

The other girls trooped out of the dining hall. Erin noticed Megan turning back to give her a curious look. But Erin just ignored it. She pretended to munch on her roll for as long as Ms. Winkle and the movie man were in the mess hall.

But the minute they got up to leave, Erin jumped up, too. It was time to be seriously bold. That director might think she was a sweet girl now, but in a couple of minutes, he was going to find out that she was also a great actress.

Erin dashed out of the dining hall behind Ms. Winkle and the man. "Excuse me," she called out. When they turned around, Erin smiled sweetly. "Do you have just one second to listen to something?"

Before they could answer, Erin struck her pose. She thrust the back of her hand across her forehead and tried to look like a woman in love.

"Romeo, Romeo, wherefore art thou Romeo?

33

Deny thy father and refuse thy name . . ."

Erin soared through the entire speech without forgetting a single word. When it was over, she batted her eyelashes at the man. "I hope you enjoyed that," she said.

"Uh, um, very much," the man said, looking bewildered.

"Ever since I starred in the Sunnyside Spectacular, I've been very interested in acting," she explained. It would help if he thought she had a background in theater.

"That's wonderful, dear," Ms. Winkle said, looking at her a little oddly. "I enjoyed your monologue very much. And my brother loves the theater. In fact, he was just stopping off here at camp on his way to New York—he's going to be seeing quite a few Broadway shows. Aren't you, George?"

The man smiled. "I try to get to as many productions as I can."

Her brother?! Erin felt her cheeks turn into hot, burning lava.

"See you later, dear," Ms. Winkle said.

Erin swallowed hard and managed to say a quick good-bye to the camp director and her brother. Then she ran all the way to the cabin as quickly as she could. The sooner she forgot what had just happened, the better.

* * *

That afternoon, when the girls went to the stables, they were surprised to see cabin four girls saddling up.

Their counselor turned to the cabin six girls with an apologetic smile. "Girls, if you wait here by the corral, we'll only be a short while," she explained. "We were scheduled for swimming, but they're fixing the swim dock. We didn't realize you were scheduled for the horses."

"It's okay," said Trina, trying to make the counselor feel better about the mix-up. "We don't mind waiting."

Speak for yourself, Erin thought as she leaned up against the corral.

Just then, Ms. Winkle and her brother, and a woman Erin had never seen before, came strolling down the path. When they saw the girls from cabin six lined up against the corral, they waved and started walking over.

"Who's that?" Katie asked, squinting into the sun as the grown-ups approached.

"The man is Ms. Winkle's brother," Erin told her. "That woman must be his wife."

"Hello, girls!" called Ms. Winkle. "Is there a line for the horses today?"

"Not a long one," Megan offered, smiling.

"I wish they had horses at the camp I went to when I was a kid," the woman said with a little laugh. "I would have loved that." She had curly black hair and wore sunglasses.

Where were the movie people now? Erin wondered. If only she could sneak away from everybody and look for them! But how could she with Ms. Winkle standing right there?

"Is this your first year at Camp Sunnyside?" the woman asked them.

"No, it's our fourth," Katie answered. "We've shared the same cabin all four years, too!"

"That's wonderful," the woman said.

What was so wonderful about it, Erin thought. Next year she was going to get down on her knees and beg her parents not to send her back here.

"What are your names, girls?" the woman asked, smiling.

"I'm Katie," Katie said. "This is Trina, and Sarah, and Megan, and Erin." She pointed to them one by one.

"Hi," they chorused. Erin just nodded. Why did she have to be stuck here talking to Ms. Winkle's sister-in-law at the same time that a film crew was at Camp Sunnyside?

"Do you ride horses at home?" the woman asked.

Megan was giggling that stupid giggle of hers. "When I was little, I thought my sheepdog was a horse, so I tried to ride him," she was telling the woman.

"Your horses are ready!" the cabin four counselor called out as she led her group of nine-year-olds out of the corral gate. "Thanks for waiting."

The girls headed toward the horses. "Nice meeting you!" Megan called out, turning back to wave at the grown-ups.

Rolling her eyes, Erin sauntered along behind the others. What was so nice about meeting *them?*

As she trotted around the ring, Erin looked all over. Where was the film crew? They weren't here at the stables. And she didn't see them down by the lake.

Wherever she went that day, she had her eyes wide open. A couple of times, she even managed to slip away from the group to do a little exploring. But she had no luck. The movie crew was nowhere to be found.

It was just another boring day at Camp Sunnyside. Except that it was worse than most days, because she had to listen to Katie running on and on about Rod Laney. And it was always the same old boring stuff. How handsome he was, and what a good actor, and how Katie wished she could see him in person and get his autograph.

Even though it was the middle of summer, Erin wished she could whip out a pair of earmuffs whenever Katie started talking about him. Not that Katie was wrong about the star. Erin had to admit he was a pretty cool actor.

But Katie didn't seem to understand that it was childish to gush. Fans should be a little cooler than that.

After dinner, Erin hurried back to the cabin so that she could spend some time boning up on her *Romeo and Juliet* piece. Even if she hadn't had a chance to show her stuff to the movie people today, tomorrow was another day. Anything could happen. She wanted to make sure she was ready.

Flopping onto the bed, she tried to shut out the chatter of her cabin mates and concentrate on Shakespeare's immortal words.

"Romeo, doff thy name—" What in the world did *doff* mean, anyway? Not knowing what the words meant made it harder to remember the speech.

Carolyn stuck her head out her door. "Okay, girls, it's almost lights out," she announced. "Sarah, remember, no reading in bed tonight."

Sarah looked surprised. "Who, me?" she said innocently.

"Who else? You're the only reading addict in this cabin." Then she noticed Erin. "Unless your habit has become contagious. Erin, are you still reading *Romeo and Juliet?*"

"It's a great play," Erin replied.

"Yes," Carolyn said dryly. "So I've heard. By the way, Megan, I have some news for you."

Something about the way she said it got all

the girls' attention. "Do you remember meeting a woman at the stables today?"

Megan nodded. Carolyn continued, "She was the casting director of the movie."

Erin gasped out loud. *The casting director?* Erin thought wildly. Oh, no! How could I have been so stupid? Why, oh why wasn't I nicer to her?

"The casting director?" Megan said with a gulp.

"Yes." Carolyn nodded. "And she wants to use you as an extra in the movie."

Katie, Trina, and Sarah all gasped. Megan just stood there, looking bewildered.

"That's great!" Trina squealed.

"Megan, you're going to be famous!" Katie shrieked.

"Forget Rod Laney," Sarah joked. "Can I have *your* autograph, Megan?"

Megan looked at all her friends as if she didn't quite understand what was happening. Then a huge grin spread across her face. "They want me to be in the movie?" she repeated. "Why me?"

"I guess you just have star quality," Carolyn said with a smile. "They want to meet with you tomorrow during free period."

Erin couldn't believe what she was hearing. Of all the girls in cabin six, Megan was the most immature. And a major space cadet! And she had that awful red hair that always frizzed up on humid days. How could the movie people have picked *her* and not Erin? She forced a smile. "Congratulations."

Katie and Trina started shrieking all over again, and Sarah grabbed Megan and gave her a huge hug.

"I can't believe it!" Megan shouted happily. "I'm going to be a movie star!"

"Come on, guys—lights out. Even for you movie stars," Carolyn added. And she went back into her room.

Still beaming, Megan managed to get her teeth brushed before she climbed into her bed and lay down. "I'll never be able to sleep tonight," she said. "Never."

In the darkness, Katie started to giggle. "Maybe you'll have to kiss Rod Laney, Megan," she said. "Wouldn't that be fabulous?"

"Yeah," Megan said, sighing happily.

"What do extras *do,* anyway?" Sarah asked.

"Beats me," Megan said.

"I'm really happy for you, Megan," Erin said. "Too bad you'll have to miss tennis, though."

"Why will she have to miss tennis?" Trina asked, yawning.

"Because of rehearsals, of course," Erin said knowingly. "Extras have lots of rehearsals."

"How do you know?" Katie asked, rubbing her eyes sleepily.

40

"Oh, I . . . read it somewhere," Erin lied. "It'll probably be so boring for you, Megan."

"Well, that's okay," Megan said. "I guess a person only gets one chance to be a movie star. I mean, I can always play tennis, right?"

Erin didn't answer. She just lay there in bed, gritting her teeth.

"Oh!" Megan breathed. "And I promise I'll try to get Rod Laney's autograph for you, Katie."

Katie didn't reply. "Katie?" Megan repeated. "She's asleep," Sarah said, in a drowsy voice.

"Wait'll I tell my friends back home about this," Megan said. "They're going to flip. Remember that movie we went to last year, Trina, and you said I looked just like the star?"

Erin looked over at Trina's bunk. "She's asleep, too," she said quietly. "So is Sarah."

"Gee. I'm never going to fall asleep, Erin. This is so incredible, isn't it? I mean, this is the best thing that ever happened to me in my whole life!"

Erin slipped out of bed and walked over to Megan's bunk. "I know," she said, sitting down next to her. "You're so lucky, Megan! And just think, you get to say all those *lines.*"

"What lines?" Megan gasped. "I'm just an extra, remember? I'm not going to have lines—am I?"

"Of course you will," Erin said. "That's why

41

they call them "extras," silly. Because they give them all the extra lines." She figured Megan was just naive enough to believe that.

"Oh," Megan said. Her smile disappeared. "But I hate learning lines."

"Don't worry. You'll do fine," Erin told her. "Remember how great you were in the Sunnyside Spectacular?"

Megan shuddered. "I remember Katie had to whisper all my lines from offstage because I kept forgetting them."

"That's okay," Erin said. "You were still great."

Megan didn't respond.

"And I could, uh, *help* you with your lines, if you want," Erin offered sweetly.

"You could? Gee, thanks, Erin." Megan sounded relieved.

"And even if the director has to yell at you a little bit, it's no big deal," Erin said. "It's worth it to be a movie star, right?"

Erin let out a big yawn. She stood up and walked over to her bed. "Well, you'd better get your beauty sleep, Megan. Good night."

"Good night," Megan said in a small voice.

Snuggling under the blanket, Erin had to stifle a giggle. Megan hated being yelled at more than anything. And memorizing lines was sheer agony for her.

42

Just as Erin was starting to drift off, a sudden shriek jerked her fully awake.

"No! No!" Megan moaned. "Don't yell—I—I can't remember it!"

Erin opened her eyes and sat up on her elbows. In the moonlight, she saw that Katie, Trina, and Sarah were still sleeping like stones. She got up and went to Megan's bed.

"Megan! Shhh!" Erin said. "What's wrong?"

Megan's eyes popped open and she sat up. "Oh, Erin! I just had the most awful nightmare! I was trying to learn my lines, and I couldn't, and this movie director with a big megaphone started yelling at me, and somebody put me in a box and they shut the lid and—oh! It was awful!"

"Come on, calm down," Erin said. "You were just dreaming."

"I know," Megan said. "But it felt so real—"

"You're really scared about being in the movie, aren't you?"

Megan bit her lip and nodded.

Erin bit *her* lip to keep herself from smiling. "Maybe you should tell them you can't do it," she suggested.

"How can I do that?" Megan asked. "They need me!"

"Just get somebody to take your place," Erin said with a casual shrug.

43

"Really?" Megan said, her eyes brightening a little in the moonlight.

"Sure. I bet you could find somebody to take your place if you try hard enough. It would have to be somebody who could memorize lines, though. And somebody who was a good actress—"

"Like who?" Megan asked.

Erin rolled her eyes. *Like me, you nit,* she thought. *What other great actresses do you know?*

"Oh, I don't know, Megan," she said out loud. Then she sat up and snapped her fingers. "Wait—I've got it!" Erin grasped Megan's arm. "Why don't *I* take your place?"

Megan sat bolt upright, rising to the bait. "Erin, what a great idea. You'd be perfect!"

"Me?" said Erin, doing her best to sound surprised. "Gosh, Megan, if you really want me to—"

"Oh, I do! I do!" Megan pleaded. "You'd be so much better than me!"

Erin couldn't argue with that. "Okay, Megan," she agreed. "Since you're such a close friend, I'll help you out. Tomorrow, *I'll* go meet with the movie people for you."

Gladly.

Chapter 4

"Okay, girls! That's all for today!" The archery counselor blew his whistle, and Erin's heart started thumping madly. It was free period—time to change her clothes and go meet the movie people!

Stepping off the archery range, she quickly put her bow and arrow in the equipment box.

"Hey Erin—Trina and I are going to the canteen for free period," Katie said. "Want to come? We could get sundaes."

"Can't," Erin said. "I'm doing something for Megan."

Katie looked surprised. "What?"

"I don't want to be in the movie," Megan said, stepping up behind Katie. "Erin's going to take my place."

"Why?" Trina asked.

"I don't want to be in the movie," Megan re-

45

peated. "I don't have time to learn lines and everything. I want to play tennis and have fun."

Erin shrugged. "She begged me to take her place, so I'm going to do it."

Sarah looked suspicious. "Are you sure you can do that?"

"Of course I can," Erin said. "That's what friends are for. Right, Megan?"

Megan hunched her shoulders and nodded, but she didn't look totally sure.

Erin ignored Katie's hard look. *"Ciao!"* she said, turning and walking away. *Ciao* was an Italian word for good-bye. It sounded like "chow." That was what Marcia always said when she was going someplace.

As soon as she turned onto the path, Erin started running. She didn't have a lot of time to get ready. Carolyn had said the movie people would be in Ms. Winkle's office all during free period, but that Megan shouldn't keep them waiting.

Hurrying to the cabin, Erin ran over what she had to do. First, take a shower. Then, get dressed. Then, put on makeup.

After her shower, Erin dried off and put on clean underwear. Then, she flung her bureau drawer open and took out her hair dryer and a brush. She blew her hair dry, coaxing it into a sophisticated wave that fell over one eye.

But it wasn't quite right.

Rummaging in her top drawer, she found the big black hair comb that was decorated with spangly black lace. Giving her reflection a sexy smile, she lifted one side of her hair in the comb and anchored it in place. The effect was perfect. Sophisticated and hip at the same time.

Now, for clothes. No way was she going to meet the movie people wearing regulation shorts and tee shirt. She pushed her Camp Sunnyside shirts aside and lifted out her skinny red halter.

In the next drawer was a pair of super-tight black bicycle shorts. They would go great with the snakeskin sandals she'd managed to pack while her mother's back was turned.

Erin put the clothes on and checked herself out in the mirror. Her hair looked good, and so did the clothes. All she needed now was some makeup, and today called for the works. Starting with a jet-black eyeliner, Erin applied mascara, smoke-gray eye shadow, snow-frost highlighter for her eyelids, cherry-pink blusher, and light red lipstick that matched the bright color of her halter.

When she was finished, she stepped back from the mirror and took another look. Pretty devastating. All she needed was a little jewelry. The string of red beads, to match her top, of course. And maybe a bracelet. Maybe a couple of bracelets. Maybe *four* bracelets.

Now all she needed was earrings. Slipping on a pair of oversized onyx and rhinestone danglers that Marcia had given her for her birthday, Erin checked out her image for the last time. She looked at least fifteen, she thought with a pleased smile.

Blowing a kiss into the mirror and smiling gleefully, Erin flew out of cabin six and made for Ms. Winkle's office. When she got there, a few other campers were scattered around the room, talking to the woman Erin had met at the stables. Erin wondered whether they were in the movie. If so, they didn't look like it. They were all dressed in Camp Sunnyside tee shirts and regulation shorts.

"May I help you?" the woman asked when Erin poked her head in the door.

"Is this where the movie extras are meeting?" Erin asked, though she already knew the answer.

"Yes, it is," the woman said. "Can I help you? I'm Joanne Lewis, the casting director."

"I know," Erin said. "Hi. I'm here to be an extra."

Ms. Lewis seemed confused. She looked at Erin and then down at the clipboard she was holding. "What's your name?"

Erin cleared her throat. "Well, my name is Erin Chapman," she began.

48

"Erin Chapman?" the casting director murmured. "I don't see any Erin on the list—"

"Oh, well, actually, I'm taking Megan Lindsay's place."

"Oh, yes, Megan Lindsay." The casting director looked up and smiled. "The little red-haired girl. Where is she?"

"She asked me to take her place," Erin explained. This casting director didn't seem very bright.

"Take her place?" she repeated, looking Erin over. "Oh, no, dear. Sorry. We can only use the people we picked."

"But—"

The casting director didn't let her finish. "I'm sorry Megan doesn't want to be an extra. She had just the right look. Now, I'm afraid you'll have to leave. We're very busy."

Erin didn't say anything. She was too mad, too upset, and too humiliated. Turning on her heels, she walked out of Ms. Winkle's office and ran out of the building.

Who did that woman think she was, anyway? After all, she was just a casting director, not a real *movie* director, or even a producer. Obviously, she wasn't a very good casting director, either. If she was, she would have known right away that Erin Chapman was someone special.

Well, Erin thought as she made her way back to the cabin, she wasn't going to take this lying down. She couldn't let one stupid casting director stand between her and stardom. Erin was too good for that! And besides, there were other ways for a girl to get discovered. She'd just have to think of them.

"Anybody here?" Erin called out when she got back to the cabin. Nobody answered.

She changed back into her Sunnyside clothes and walked by Carolyn's private room on her way to the bathroom. The door was wide open.

Erin didn't mean to snoop, but who could have ignored the red and yellow Four Star production stationery sitting on top of Carolyn's desk?

Glancing over her shoulder, to make sure no one was coming, Erin stepped inside.

The production schedule! Erin snatched it up. There was today's date. Her eyes scanned the sheet. 9:00 P.M., Lakefront. Erin smiled. All she had to do now was figure out a way to sneak away from the cabin.

A voice behind her made Erin whirl around like a top.

"What are you doing in Carolyn's room?" Katie stood there, staring at her.

"Katie!" Erin exclaimed, quickly putting the Four Star paper back down on Carolyn's desk. "I'm so glad it's only you!"

Katie narrowed her eyes. "What's that? And why are you here?"

"Wait till I tell you what I just found out!"

Erin said, grabbing Katie by the arm and leading her out of the room. "The film crew is going to be down at the lake tonight!"

Katie looked at Erin suspiciously. "So?" she asked.

"So? You want to see Rod Laney up close, don't you?"

It took Katie only a second to figure out what Erin was getting at. Her eyes lit up. "Are you saying we should go down to the lake tonight?"

"*I'm* going," Erin said. "You can come with me if you want to."

The "if" was totally unnecessary.

That night, without saying anything to the other girls of cabin six, Erin and Katie began stuffing their beds with pillows to make it seem like they were lying in them.

"What's going on?" Trina asked, sounding alarmed.

"Oh, nothing," Erin said breezily.

Trina shot a quick glance at Katie. "Katie," she said, her voice firmer this time. "What are you doing?"

Katie seemed nervous. Erin could tell she was working hard to control her giggling. "Oh, nothing," she said, trying to shrug her shoulders casually. "Erin and I are just—um, we're going out for a little walk. That's all."

"Going out?" Sarah looked up from her book.

51

"If you go out now, you're going to get into trouble! Big trouble!"

"No, we're not. We're just going for a walk," Erin repeated. "Don't get so upset."

"But we're not supposed to leave the cabin after eight-thirty," Trina reminded them. "You know that."

"We know a lot of things," Erin said. "Right, Katie?"

Katie looked over at Trina and promised, "It'll be okay. If Carolyn comes in she'll think we're in bed sleeping." Katie gave the pillows under her blanket one last pat.

"Come on, Katie," said Erin, who was already at the door with her flashlight. "Bye, girls!"

Outside, Erin and Katie had to cover their mouths to keep from laughing. It felt so good to be out of the cabin and on their way to a great adventure!

"When we get there, let's split up," Erin whispered as they made their way across the lawn that led down to the lake.

"Why?" Katie asked, sounding just the least bit hurt.

"Because you want to see Rod Laney, and I want to find out who the director is," Erin explained.

"Look! See that light? They're making the movie right over there!" Katie squealed.

"Shhhh!" Erin warned. "We're not supposed to be here, remember?"

"Oh, no!" Katie shrieked. "I forgot a pen!"

"Shhh!" Erin said again, louder this time.

"But how am I going to get Rod Laney's autograph if I don't have a pen?" Katie wailed.

They were almost at the shoreline now. "Will you be quiet!" Erin scolded in a raspy whisper. A ring of people stood facing the lake. A bunch of giant lights on poles were aimed out onto the water, where a little boat floated with two people in it.

"Quiet, please," a man called out as Katie and Erin crept closer to the people. "We're rolling—"

Erin strained her eyes to see who the director might be. Would he be the man behind the camera? Or was that the cameraman? It was hard to tell in the moonlight. None of the movie people seemed to be doing anything much.

Then Katie's fingers dug into her arm. "I think I see him! I think I see him!" Katie whispered hysterically.

Erin panicked. Why couldn't Katie just shut up?

"I wonder if that's Rod Laney in the boat?" said Katie.

They were crouched down now, only a few feet from the film crew. Above them, the moon shone on the lake and a soft breeze rustled through the trees. It was all so perfect.

That is, it was perfect until Erin felt a huge hand on her shoulder. She whirled around and found herself staring into the eyes of a big, rough-looking man.

"Are you with the movie?" he asked.

"Y-yes," Erin lied. "We're, um, extras."

Hearing this, Katie spun around, too. A look of frozen terror was on her face. "Oh, hi," she gulped.

The man sighed. "Nice try, girls. But I'm afraid I can't let you stay here."

"But we're extras!" Erin protested.

"We're not using any extras tonight, honey," he told her. "Now shall I call a counselor to take you back to your cabin? Or can you get back by yourselves?"

Erin hung her head. "We'll go by ourselves," she said with a discouraged sigh.

"Rats!" said Katie as they headed back to the cabin. "Now I'll never get to meet Rod Laney."

"Don't be so sure of that," Erin said, squinting her eyes as she racked her brain for a plan. "There has to be another way," she said softly, "and I'm going to find it."

Chapter 5

The next day at breakfast, Ms. Winkle went to the front of the dining hall for the morning announcements. "Girls! Girls!" she said loudly. "May I have your attention, please?"

As the noise died down, Erin turned toward the front and noticed that the camp director wasn't smiling. In fact, she looked unusually stern.

"It has been brought to my attention," Ms. Winkle began, pausing for what seemed to be dramatic effect, "that two girls were out after hours last night and went to the lakefront where the film crew was working." A murmur went through the room. Erin could have sworn she detected a note of admiration in it.

"I don't know who they were," Ms. Winkle continued, "but we simply cannot tolerate that kind of behavior. The movie people have a big job to do while they're here, and the fewer distractions they have, the better they'll be able to do it. I asked you once, and I must ask you again *not* to interfere in their work! Now, I hope I won't have to mention this again. Enjoy your breakfasts." With that, Ms. Winkle returned to her table, and an excited buzz filled the room.

Suddenly, Trina and Sarah and Megan were all staring suspiciously at Erin and Katie. Katie's face had turned bright red.

"Katie," Trina said in a voice that was all business. "She's talking about you and Erin, right?"

Katie shifted uncomfortably in her seat. Erin could tell that she didn't want to lie to her best friend. But fortunately, Carolyn came along at that moment. "Hi," she said. "How's breakfast?"

Erin sighed with relief. One thing about the girls of cabin six: They were loyal. There was no way Carolyn would ever find out from any of them what had happened last night.

"Yuck," said Megan, looking down at her breakfast tray. "I hate oatmeal. It's so mushy."

"I love oatmeal," Sarah said, pouring milk over hers. "It reminds me of winter. You know, sitting by a warm fire with a good book."

"Nobody likes oatmeal, Sarah," Katie said, shaking her head. "You're weird."

"That's not a nice thing to say," Carolyn remarked.

"I guess Katie's been hanging around with Erin too much," Sarah muttered, almost under her breath.

Erin shot her a withering look. Katie stuck out her tongue. Carolyn surveyed them all with narrowed eyes. "What's going on?"

"Sorry, Sarah," Katie said. "I'm just in a bad mood."

"Maybe you didn't get enough sleep last night," Megan said with a twinkle in her eyes.

"I'm going for some more juice," Carolyn said after a couple of minutes. "Anybody else want some?"

"No, thank you," said Trina. The other girls just shook their heads. Carolyn got up and walked away from the table.

The minute she was gone, Trina turned to Katie with a reproving look. "You don't have to keep secrets from me."

"Who said I was keeping a secret from you?" Katie mumbled.

"Is your counselor here?" Erin looked up and saw the casting director with some papers in her hand.

"She went to get something," Erin said. She bestowed her most charming smile on the woman. "Can we help you?"

The casting director handed her a sheet of paper. "Would you give this to her?" Then her eyes lit on Megan. "Dear, I'm so sorry you decided not to be an extra. We could really use you in a scene this morning."

Megan fidgeted.

"Why don't you do it, Megan?" Sarah urged.

Megan gazed at the woman anxiously. "Would I have to learn any lines?"

"Good heavens, no," she said. "You'll just be part of a crowd."

Megan brightened. "I guess I can handle that."

"Great," the casting director said. "Come to the activities hall right after breakfast, all right?"

As soon as she left, Megan began bouncing up and down. "I'm going to be in a movie! I'm going to be in a movie!"

Erin tried to look disinterested. Then, under the table, she studied the paper the woman had handed her.

"What is it?" Katie asked.

"Oh, nothing important," Erin said. It was the day's shooting schedule. Luckily, Erin had a good memory.

She put the paper facedown by Carolyn's place setting and announced, "I'm going to the girls' room. Anybody want to come?" She gave Katie a meaningful look.

Katie leaped up like a kangaroo. "Yeah, I'll come."

When they were far enough away from the

table so that the others couldn't hear, Erin began whispering her plan to Katie. Katie practically started jumping up and down when she heard it. "Erin, you're a genius!" she said in an excited whisper.

Erin considered that. "You're probably right."

The arts and crafts cabin was bustling with activity. A few days earlier, the girls had started making what Donna, the arts and crafts counselor, called junk collages. They were creations made from buttons, old jewelry, paper clips, macaroni, anything the girls could get their hands on. Erin thought the whole concept was ridiculously infantile. And she was sick of hearing Megan talk about her experience as an extra.

"It was so neat!" she kept saying. "They put makeup on us, and there were cameras and lights and the director said things like 'take one' and 'take two' and 'cut'!"

"What did you have to do?" Trina asked.

"Just sit around and pretend we were talking to each other."

"Did you see Rod Laney?" Katie asked.

"No, there weren't any stars around. But it was fun anyway."

Donna came around to look at their work. "Megan, a seascape! I love it!"

"If you blow on the feathers, it makes it look

59

like the water is moving," Megan explained, demonstrating.

"Very creative," Donna said, patting Megan on the shoulder.

When the counselor came to Erin, she squinted her eyes. She looked like she was trying very hard to concentrate. "Hmmmmm . . ." she said. "Were you trying for something specific? Or were you just making up a design?"

Erin shrugged. "Just making up a design, I guess."

Donna looked at Erin's piece again and nodded. "Okay," she said.

"Donna?" Erin said, before the counselor went on to Katie. "I'm—ugh—I'm—"

"What's the matter, Erin?" Donna asked, a look of alarm on her face.

"I'm getting these terrible—ugh—pains." Erin put down the glitter she had in her hand and doubled over with a grunt.

"Me, too!" cried Katie, who wasn't nearly as good an actress. "My stomach really hurts. I think it was that oatmeal. It made me sick."

"Oh, no," Megan said, looking concerned. "You look terrible."

"I've got to lie down a minute," Erin said, making her breathing sound as labored as possible.

"Me, too," Katie said, imitating Erin.

From the corner of her eye, Erin noticed Trina

and Sarah giving them disapproving looks. But even if they suspected the girls were faking, Erin knew they wouldn't say anything. The cabin six loyalty would protect them.

"Maybe I'd better walk you over to the infirmary," Donna suggested, looking the two girls over.

"You don't have to come with us, Donna," Erin said in a pitiful voice. "We can get there by ourselves."

Katie nodded, and then let out a groan that made it sound like she was dying.

"No, I want to go with you," Donna said. "Let me tell the other girls, though."

Across the room, two girls from cabin four let out a shriek. "Oh, no!" one of them cried. "I dropped the glue!"

"It's all over my shoes!" the other one said.

"Hey, that's *my* glue," a third girl shouted. "Donna, she took my glue, and now it's all over the floor."

"What a mess," Donna said, hurrying over to the younger girls. "We have to clean this up before it dries." With a distracted wave in Erin's direction, she said, "You two will have to go to the infirmary yourselves, okay? I've got to take care of this."

"Okay, Donna," Erin said. Still bent over, she and Katie walked toward the door.

As they passed Megan, she said, "Hey, are you guys all right?"

Megan looked so worried that Erin nearly told her the truth. "We'll talk to you later, Megan," she said instead, hustling Katie out the door. When they were a short distance away, Erin glanced back to see if Donna was watching them. She wasn't.

"Okay! Let's go!" Erin shouted, suddenly standing up straight and dashing toward the pool.

There was nobody at the pool. "It isn't time yet," Erin said, checking her expensive watch. "I'd better take this off." She slipped off the watch and put it inside one of the sneakers she'd also taken off. "You hide behind that tree," she told Katie, pointing to a large pine just outside the fence around the pool.

"Okay," Katie agreed, her face glowing with excitement.

"Don't worry. This is going to work like a charm," Erin assured her. "You're going to get to meet Rod Laney, and I'm going to get a part in the movie!"

"Right!" said Katie, brightening a little.

"But, remember," Erin emphasized, "as soon as they come—"

"You mean, as soon as *Rod Laney* comes," Katie corrected her.

"Right," said Erin. "As soon as Rod Laney comes, it's all systems go!"

"Oh, this is so fabulous!" Katie said before she slipped around the fence and went to hide.

Erin took a deep breath and sauntered over to the edge of the pool. Aware that at any minute the movie director might be looking at her, she eased herself down gingerly, and began dangling her feet in the water. Every so often, she stole a quick glance behind her to see if anyone was coming.

After a few minutes, she saw two men she'd never seen before approaching the pool area on her left. They had to be the director and producer! Why else would they be the first ones there?

When they were about fifty feet away, Erin slid off the edge of the pool and started splashing wildly. "Help!" she cried. "Help! I'm drowning!"

Before the men could reach Erin, Katie ran out from behind the pine tree and raced to the pool's edge. "Don't worry!" she shouted. "I'll save you!" Then she dove into the water.

The men trotted to the pool and watched in amazement as Katie pulled her bigger friend out of the water. Erin didn't make Katie's job easy, either. She was too busy screaming hysterically and thrashing around as she pretended to drown.

At last, Katie hauled Erin out of the pool and laid her down in a lounge chair. "Are you okay?" asked one of the men, a dark-haired guy with a small mustache. Erin figured he was the movie director—they always wore mustaches— and his companion was probably the producer. But of course, it might have been the other way around. The second guy had long blond hair tied up in a ponytail—very artistic.

"Good work, honey," the man with the pony-tail told Katie.

"Guess what?" Erin said brightly as she sat up suddenly. "I wasn't really drowning!"

"What?" the man with the mustache gasped.

"What *were* you doing?" the blond man said with a confused look in his blue eyes.

"Acting!" Erin announced with a triumphant gleam in her eyes.

"Hey, a stunt like that could be dangerous," the blond man said.

"The thing is," Erin proclaimed earnestly, "I want to act with all my heart and soul. I want to act more than anything in the entire world!"

"A lot of people want to act. That doesn't give them a right to pull a stunt like that," the dark-haired man told her.

"But I figured if the director and the producer saw me act, they'd want to put me in the movie," Erin said. "That's why I did it. For you."

The dark-haired man shook his head. "Number one," he said, "we're not the director and the producer. We're electricians. Number two, no one is allowed in this area right now except the cast and crew. Got it?"

Erin wanted to kick herself. How could she have been so stupid? "Can't you talk to the director or the producer for me?" she said, trying not to sound like she was begging.

"If you don't leave the area right away, we're going to have to contact the counselors," the blond man warned.

"Okay," Erin said, wishing she could just sink into the earth. She turned to Katie, who had a stunned expression on her face. "Let's go."

"Nice work, Erin," Katie said bitterly when they were out of the pool area.

"Don't blame me!" Erin protested. "How was I supposed to know they were only electricians?"

Katie snorted. "You said you were going to wait till you saw Rod Laney, remember? That's the only reason I was here! If he saw me making the rescue, then he'd think I was a heroine. He might even have kissed me!"

"I thought one of those men *was* Rod Laney, Katie," Erin insisted. It was an out-and-out lie, but she usually lied well. Unfortunately, not this time.

"Oh, come on," Katie stormed. "Rod Laney is

65

tall and handsome. Those guys were just okay-looking!"

"Sorry," Erin shrugged. "I made a mistake."

"I'll say," Katie huffed.

"Well, you don't have to get mad," Erin said as she picked up her watch and shoes.

Katie shot her a look of pure poison. "I'm wet," she muttered, "and hungry, too. We're missing lunch."

"Let's go then," Erin said. "We'll have to hide these wet clothes so Carolyn doesn't see them; then we can go to lunch."

"I don't know why I ever listen to you," Katie muttered under her breath as they walked back to the cabin.

Erin said nothing.

Without speaking, the two girls walked back to the cabin, changed into dry clothes, and hid their wet ones at the bottom of the clothing hamper. Then, they headed to the dining hall. If they were lucky, there would still be some lunch left.

"Who's that?" Katie wondered aloud as they approached the hall. A girl about their age was hanging around out front. The girl was exceptionally pretty, with pale blonde hair and wide green eyes.

"She must be a day camper," Erin said.

The two girls approached the stranger. "Day campers are supposed to stay with their group,"

Katie told the girl firmly. "Those are the rules here."

"Really?" the girl said with a trace of sarcasm.

"Ms. Winkle doesn't want anybody getting lost or wandering around. Day campers are supposed to stay with their group at all times. You'd better come into the dining hall or you could get in big trouble." Typical Katie, Erin thought. Always wants to be the boss.

But Katie seemed to have met her match in the pretty blonde girl she was talking to. "Thanks for the information," the girl shot back. "But I'm not a 'day camper,' whatever that is. I happen to be a professional actress. And I'm not here at this camp for fun and games. I'm in the film, for your information."

Katie seemed to be taken aback by the girl's snotty tone. When she recovered, she delivered a parting shot. "Well, I guess we should be honored by your presence. C'mon, Erin. Let's go."

"Not yet," Erin answered sweetly. "You go on ahead, okay?"

Katie walked into the dining hall, looking back once to see what Erin was about to do. Erin gave her a little wave. When Katie was gone, Erin turned to the actress.

"My name is Erin Chapman," she said. "What's yours?"

"Tish Lambert," the girl answered, almost unwillingly. "What are you hanging around here for? I'm not lost or anything."

"I'm not standing here because of you," Erin protested. "I'm just not that hungry."

"Yeah, right," Tish drawled. "Don't you think I know you want to talk to me because I'm in the movie?"

"You mean the movie they're making here?" Erin asked innocently. "Oh, yes. I heard about that."

"Give me a break. You think that if you talk to me maybe you'll get to meet Rod Laney. Or else you think I'll introduce you to the casting director, or something," Tish said smugly. "It's been happening ever since we got here."

"Who's Rod Laney?" Erin asked.

"Oh, come on," Tish said. "Everybody knows who Rod Laney is!"

"Oh, right!" Erin said, bringing her palm to her forehead. "He's an actor! I never saw him in anything, but I heard he's pretty good."

Tish cast a wary look at Erin, who smiled sweetly. "Frankly, he's not that good an actor," Tish said. "He's more like a hunk who got lucky."

"What's the name of the movie you're working on?" Erin asked.

"The Camp Capers," Tish answered. "Isn't that stupid? I mean, it's so cutesy I could puke. I hope they change it."

"It is kind of cutesy," Erin agreed. "Is it a good script?"

Tish gave Erin a withering stare. "What do you think? I mean, with a name like that, how good could it be? But it'll probably be a big box-office success. Herb Ritter's films always are. Since he stopped acting and started directing teen films, all his movies have made a ton of money."

"Gosh," Erin said, hoping she sounded appropriately impressed. "You're lucky! It must be so much fun being in a movie!"

Tish looked at Erin as if she were out of her mind. "Fun? Are you crazy! It's awful! Half the time you just stand around and wait, wait, wait, and the other half you have to memorize a bunch of stupid lines. And the way they treat you? It's horrible. Herb thinks the way to get a good performance from actors is to yell at them. And to the crew, actors are just so many pieces of furniture!"

"Gosh," said Erin, as sympathetically as she could muster. Obviously, this girl had a pretty bad attitude problem. But it didn't mean she couldn't be useful. . . .

"You sound like you need a break," Erin began.

But before she could finish, a young woman with a ponytail—clipboard tucked under her arm—came running up the path. "Tish!" she snapped. "What are you doing here? Everybody is looking for you!"

"I was standing around waiting for so long, I thought I'd take a walk around the camp," Tish replied. "I mean, if the lighting people would get their act together for a change, it would really be great."

"Herb told you it would be awhile," the woman stressed. "He told you to stick around."

"What's the difference? With the size of my role I could disappear for two weeks and it wouldn't matter."

"Get back to the set immediately," the woman ordered. "Herb's about to go on the warpath."

Tish let out a deep, mournful sigh and turned to Erin. "And you thought I was lucky. You're the one who gets to play." She turned to go.

"Wait!" said Erin, following her down the path a short way. Making sure the woman was out of earshot, she whispered, "I just got a great idea! Why don't you sneak away from the movie crew tonight and come to my cabin? We always have a blast after lights-out."

"Tish! Let's go!" the woman called.

Tish thought about it. "Maybe I will," she said. "It couldn't be any more boring than what I've been doing."

"It's cabin six," Erin told her. "I'll be waiting!"

The actress took off. Erin smiled as she watched the departing figure. So Tish thought all Erin did was play. Well, that was just fine. As long as she believed that, Tish wouldn't be able to figure out what Erin was really up to.

Chapter 6

Erin raced to the dining hall. The only thing left for lunch was a pathetic-looking portion of macaroni and cheese. But Erin didn't mind. She had more important things to think about than food.

"That girl was really obnoxious!" Katie said when Erin walked up to the table and took her seat.

"What girl?" Megan wanted to know.

"Her name is Tish Lambert," Erin told Megan. "She's an actress who's working on the film."

Megan's eyes widened. "Really? How'd you meet her?"

"She was just standing around outside, and we started talking," Erin said.

"She's real snobby," Katie said. "Ultra in love with herself. I could just tell."

"I thought she was okay," Erin said, spread-

72

ing butter on a roll. "In fact, I invited her to our cabin tonight."

"You—what?" Katie stared at her in astonishment.

"I invited her to our cabin," Erin repeated. "I thought she'd enjoy seeing how we live."

Katie glared at her. "You might have asked *us* first, before you invited her. I guarantee, no one's going to like her any more than I do."

Erin glared right back. "You want to meet Rod Laney, don't you?"

"Of course. But what does that have to do with—" Katie stopped, and clapped her hand to her mouth.

Erin nodded. "Exactly. If we buddy up to Tish, you can get her to introduce you."

Katie looked uncomfortable. "That's using people."

"So what?" Erin leaned back in her chair. "We're not hurting anybody."

Sarah let out a sigh. "You guys are really going off the deep end. I'm going back to the cabin to read," she said.

"I'll go with you," Megan told her.

When they were gone, Trina said, "I don't think that's very nice, Erin."

She's such a goody-goody, Erin thought. "We're not *using* her, okay? We're just being friendly."

73

"But I'll bet you wouldn't be so friendly if she wasn't an actress," Katie said.

"I might," Erin said.

"Hah," Katie shook her head. "I bet that girl doesn't have one friend in the whole world."

"All the more reason we should be nice to her. Right, Trina?" Erin said with a sweet smile.

"I guess so," Trina answered uncertainly.

All day, Erin looked forward to her meeting with Tish. The more she thought about Tish, the more she realized how helpful this girl could be—as long as she didn't figure out Erin's plan. She was going to get a part in this movie no matter what. By the time school started, she would be a local celebrity. Jessica Meyers and everyone else would die of jealousy.

"Megan," Erin complained later that evening. "Could you get this junk up off the floor?"

"I'm writing a letter," Megan said. Megan had been sitting in a chair with a pencil in her mouth, staring off into space, for at least half an hour.

"We're having company, remember?" Erin reminded her.

"Who?" Megan said, lifting her head like a dog.

"You are really hopeless," Erin muttered. She bent to the floor and picked up Megan's stuff. "Where does this go?"

Megan shrugged. "I dunno. Anywhere, I guess."

"Did you tell Carolyn we're having company?" Trina asked Erin.

"Not yet," Erin answered. "Come on, Megan. Keep picking up."

"I'll help you, Megan," Trina offered.

A knock on the door interrupted them. Carolyn came out of her room and went to open it.

It was Darrell. "Ms. Winkle's called an emergency counselor's meeting," he told Carolyn. "She wants us to meet in her office right away."

Carolyn turned to the girls. "Will you be okay staying here by yourselves for a while?"

What kind of question was that? Erin wondered. Carolyn must have thought they were all five years old.

"What's the matter?" Trina asked the two counselors.

Darrell shook his head. "I don't really know what it's about. But I've got to let Donna know, too. Meet me in front of cabin four, Carolyn."

"Okay," Carolyn murmured as Darrell left. "I'd better bring a sweater and my flashlight," she said, walking into her room to get them.

"Shouldn't we tell her someone is coming over?" Trina asked.

"What for?" Erin said.

Carolyn stepped back into the room, wearing her red sweater and holding the flashlight.

75

"Okay, guys, I'm gone. Hold down the fort till I get back, okay?"

Hold down the fort? Erin's eyes rolled up to the ceiling. Carolyn was a complete cornball.

Only seconds after she left, there was a knock at the door.

"That must be Tish," Erin said, pulling the door open. "Hi, Tish!"

"Why didn't you tell me this shack was out in the boonies? I almost got lost looking for it," Tish complained as she stepped into the cabin.

"Tish, I'd like you to meet my cabin mates. You already met Katie," Erin began.

"Hi," Katie said, trying to smile.

"And this is Trina, and Megan, and Sarah." One after another, the girls said hi. Tish looked them over like a queen reviewing her troops. "Hi," she said with a nod.

"Are you really an actress?" Megan blurted out, looking at the pretty girl.

"No," Tish answered, her voice dripping with sarcasm. "I'm really a space alien."

Megan looked confused. Erin laughed to try to break the tense silence. "That's cute," she told Tish. Then she turned to Megan and said, "Yes, she's an actress. She's starring in the movie they're making here."

"That must be a lot of fun," Trina offered.

"Not really," Tish said with a shrug.

"How do you like the camp?" Katie asked.

"It's really bizarre," Tish said, flopping down next to Erin. "I can't believe you all have to wear those stupid uniforms. They look really dumb."

"I know," Erin agreed.

"They're just shorts and tee shirts," Sarah said. "I kind of like them."

"I would never be seen in anything that stupid," Tish said.

"We have to wear them," Megan said. "It's the rules."

"Well, I wouldn't. I'd go on strike first."

"Then you'd be sent home," Sarah replied.

Tish snorted. "I wouldn't be here in the first place."

"So Tish, um, how's the movie going?" Erin asked.

Tish shrugged her slender shoulders. "I can't believe I'm doing this part for union minimum. My agent wanted me to do it because it's a Herb Ritter film, but it really isn't worth it."

"What's union minimum?" Megan asked.

"Oh, never mind. You wouldn't understand," Tish said, leaning back on her elbows. An uncomfortable silence followed.

"The thing that really gets me," Tish said after a while, "is the way they talk to me. It's always, 'Tish, get over here.' 'Tish, could you say that line like you really mean it?' What do they think I am? A machine?"

Erin hid a smile. From what Tish was saying, she couldn't be a very good actress. The movie people would *never* have to tell Erin to put more feeling in a line. She'd give them so much feeling the tears would be running down their cheeks!

"And then, they're always telling me to hurry up, but when I get ready to do my scene, I have to wait for everybody else! I'm really sick of making small talk with Rod Laney, too, you know? Frankly, he's not that interesting."

"He's not?" Katie said, looking incredulous.

"Oh, all the other actors like him. But they're pretty dorky, too. They act like this stupid movie is some big deal."

"Gosh, you make being in a movie sound awful," Megan said.

"Oh, it's not all bad," Tish told her. "Just most of it."

"Megan was an extra this morning," Trina told Tish.

"I'm sure you were just terrific," Tish said with a smirk.

"You know, we did a play here last month," Sarah said. "Megan was in it. So you see, she's acted before."

"Oh. Excuuuse me," Tish said, looking bored.

"Erin had a big part in it," Megan added. "She was really great, too."

Erin wished she could have strangled Megan right then and there.

Tish turned to Erin, her blonde head cocked to one side. "You were in a play?"

"It was no big deal," Erin told Tish. "You know, it's suddenly stuffy in here. I can hardly breathe. Want to take a walk, Tish?"

"Well, I probably should get back," Tish said.

"Nice meeting you," Trina said. None of the others even managed to work up the friendliness to say good-bye.

Erin opened the door and stepped outside with Tish. "Don't mind them," she said. "They probably never met a real actress before."

"It's okay," Tish said airily. "People are always jealous of me. They just don't understand how much garbage you have to put up with in the movie biz."

Erin couldn't have come up with a better lead-in if she'd planned one. "Well, why do you take it? Maybe you should think about letting them know how you feel. Maybe if you give the director a piece of your mind, things will get better," she urged. "I mean, they have no right to treat you like an idiot!"

"Ooh, I'd really love to tell the great Herb Ritter what I really think of him," Tish said, turning her face up to the night sky. "But I don't think he'd want to hear what I have to say."

"So what?" Erin said. *"You* would feel a lot better if you got some of this stuff off your chest, wouldn't you? And if he knew how you really felt, maybe he'd change."

"There's just one problem with that idea," Tish said. "He might fire me."

"No, he wouldn't! You're too talented to be fired. And besides, who could he get to replace you? I think you should threaten to quit! Then they'll have to treat you better!"

Tish looked thoughtful. "You know, what you're saying makes a lot of sense."

It certainly does, Erin thought gleefully. "By the way, where are you going to be shooting tomorrow?" Erin asked. "I thought maybe I'd drop by and watch."

"That's not a bad idea," Tish said. "Especially if I decide to tell them off. I could use some support."

"You can count on me, Tish."

Suddenly, a beam of light flashed in their eyes. Erin put the back of her hand over her eyes and tried to look out into the darkness.

"Are you Tish Lambert?" Carolyn's voice asked.

"Yes," Tish answered.

"Thank goodness!" Carolyn said, sounding very relieved. She walked up to the stoop and faced Tish. "I don't want to alarm you, but did you know that you've been officially missing for two hours? The movie people were going nuts looking for you!"

Tish got up. "Well, I'd better get back. See you tomorrow, Erin."

"Bye, Tish," said Erin. "See you tomorrow." She allowed herself a smile of satisfaction. Everything was working as planned.

Chapter 7

The next morning, Erin announced that she wasn't going to archery with the others. "I've got something else to do."

"Like what?" Megan asked.

"Tish invited me to the set today," Erin said casually.

"Wow," said Sarah, obviously impressed.

"I thought we weren't allowed to hang around the movie people," Trina said, looking worried. "Isn't it against the rules?"

Erin shrugged. "Lots of things are against the rules, Trina," she said as if she were talking to a two-year-old. "You'll find out when you grow up that there's a lot more to life than following instructions. Honestly, are we slaves around here, or what?"

Trina shook her head in dismay. "You know something, Erin, it seems to me you're heading for a lot of trouble."

Erin raised her eyes to the sky and sighed. "Don't worry about it, okay, Trina? I'm a big girl. I can handle myself."

"Oh, yeah?" Katie challenged. "And what if Carolyn asks us why you aren't at archery? Are we supposed to lie for you *again?*" Katie had walked right in front of Erin. Her hands on her hips, she blocked Erin's way.

"I'm not going to lie for you anymore, Erin," Trina said.

"Me neither," Sarah threw in.

With a wave of her hand, Erin shooed her cabin mates out of the way. They were acting like such children! "Listen, nobody has to lie for me. If anybody wants to know where I am, you can tell them the truth—that the movie people want me at the shoot." Erin started down the path to the shoot, then turned back to deliver a parting shot. "Have fun with your bows and arrows, okay?" Then, with a wave over her shoulder, she left them standing there.

The movie was filming down in the gully behind the stables. Erin saw the production truck parked on the gravel road by the corral. Stepping off the main path, she followed the sound of voices down into the gully.

There were fewer people at the shoot than there had been the other night at the lake. Erin studied the little group from behind a tall bush before venturing any closer. Tish was standing by herself, leaning against a large tree. She looked bored and frustrated. One hand was on her hip, and she was tapping her foot.

A bunch of people were standing in a ring around Tish. Erin recognized the woman with the ponytail. As usual, she had her clipboard in her hand, and she seemed to be consulting a lot with a good-looking silver-haired man. Then the man turned toward her, and Erin gasped. He was Herb Ritter, the film-star-turned-director! Erin recognized him from a million movies.

"Hi, Tish, how's it going?" A makeup lady walked up to Tish, dabbed her face with powder, and fluffed her bangs. Erin heaved a jealous sigh. It must be so great to be fussed over like that, she thought.

The silver-haired man walked over to the big guy who'd shooed Erin and Katie away from the lake that first night. "Sam, I want a tight shot on her face. Let me take a look at the picture, okay?" He bent over and looked into the camera's viewfinder. "Tish, sweetheart, can you start crying please?"

"Are we shooting?" Tish asked.

"No," Mr. Ritter said. 'I just want to see how you look in this light."

Tish made a face, but she did as she was told. Turning to the tree, and putting her arms up near her forehead, she pretended to sob.

"Tish, could you do it for real?" Mr. Ritter said. "Consider this a rehearsal."

"I've been rehearsing all morning!" Tish whined. "I'm tired of rehearsing!"

"Rehearsing is what you're being paid for," the director snapped. "Try not to forget that!"

"Stop yelling at me!" Tish shot back, her eyes blazing.

"If you wouldn't act like such a spoiled brat, I wouldn't have to yell!" the director shouted.

Tish glared at him. She put her hands on her hips and stuck her jaw out. "That's it!" she declared. "I'm not taking this anymore! You can take this movie and stuff it, because I refuse to be treated like this!"

Erin hadn't seen a good old-fashioned temper tantrum like this in a long time. And it was exactly what she wanted to see. She had all she could do to keep from applauding.

"Furthermore, I don't care about this movie! If you want to fire me, go right ahead!" Tish ranted. Then she ran off, heading for a small trailer.

Dismayed, the director watched her go. "Oh, boy," he said, running a hand through his silver hair.

The lady with the ponytail shook her head. "Here we go again."

"I'd just love to get rid of her," the director

muttered. "She's a pain in the neck, and she's not even that good."

Erin couldn't contain herself any longer. She stepped around the bush and walked over to the movie people.

"I can do her role," she said from a few feet behind the director. He turned and glanced at her blankly. Then he flopped back down in his black and white director's chair and picked up what looked like a copy of the script.

Erin cleared her throat and spoke up loudly. "I'm a very good actress, and I can do her part."

As if a mosquito were buzzing around him, the director turned and glanced at her again. From the look on his face, Erin couldn't tell what he was thinking, but she guessed he was looking her over, and she knew he had to be impressed. After all, hadn't she taken a full half hour after breakfast just to get her makeup perfect? Erin knew she was looking her gorgeous best.

She smiled at him brightly, and said, "Mr. Ritter, I just happened to be passing by, and—"

"Yes, yes, nice to meet you," he said and turned back to the script. Why wasn't he responding? Erin wondered. Hadn't he heard her?

Just then, Tish came back out of the trailer. Her expression was still stormy.

The director bounded out of his chair, clapping his hands. "Okay! Let's roll this one! Take fourteen!" he told the cameraman.

"Rolling . . . and . . . action!" said the big man.

Wordlessly, Tish went over to the tree, leaned against it, and let out some of the most heart-rending sobs Erin had ever heard.

"Nice, nice," the director murmured. "And cut!"

He walked to Tish and put an arm around her shoulders. "Good."

"Gee, thanks," Tish said, sarcasm dripping from her tongue. Then she spotted Erin. "When did you get here? I didn't even see you!"

The crew started packing up their gear, and everyone began climbing up the hill to where the truck was waiting.

The woman with the ponytail came over to the two girls. "This is Jane Truby," Tish told Erin. "She's the A.D."

"A.D.?" Erin repeated.

"Assistant Director," Tish explained. Erin smiled brightly, but the woman ignored her completely, as if she were just a bush or a piece of furniture.

"Tish, the next location is at the softball field. It's scene twenty-seven, okay? You can look it over in your script when we get there. That's the one where you win the ball game."

"Yeah, okay," Tish said, with a total lack of enthusiasm.

"Oh, and by the way," the assistant director added, "We're going to have to set up some screens because it's supposed to be a cloudy day. I hope you'll cooperate . . ."

"But that's going to take hours!" Tish complained. "I just did that other scene and now I'm supposed to go stand in the hot sun for an hour while they set up screens? Forget it!"

The woman spoke evenly. "Well, you've got to do it, Tish, because we don't have a stand-in for you."

"Well, why don't you?" Tish demanded, stamping her foot. "Don't I even rate a stand-in?"

"It wasn't in your contract," said Herb Ritter, coming up to them and smiling through gritted teeth. "Take it up with your agent."

"Well, I'm not going to stand there in the blazing sun and burn to a crisp. You just get me a stand-in, Herb!"

"Tish, I told you. We don't have a stand-in."

"Yes, you do!" Tish said, grabbing onto Erin's arm and pulling her forward. "Here she is. I want this girl to be my stand-in!"

The woman with the ponytail looked over at Herb Ritter. The director nodded thoughtfully as he looked Erin over from head to foot. Erin's heart was beating dizzily. This could be her big break after all!

"If I could have a stand-in, I wouldn't get so crabby and frustrated," Tish wheedled.

"She's the right size," the woman told the director.

Oh, please, please, say yes, Erin prayed.

And for once, her prayers were answered. "Okay," the director agreed. "It's a deal. We use this girl as your stand-in, but that means no more temper tantrums from you."

Tish grinned. "Deal!"

"You mean—?" Erin began, excitedly.

"He means you're Tish's stand-in," Jane Truby told Erin with a tired look on her face. "Do you know what you have to do?"

"Well, not really."

"Great." The assistant director sighed. "Okay, I'm going to tell you. Listen up, I'm only going to say it once." The way she explained it, the stand-in stood where the actor would be standing during filming. The lighting people would use her to adjust their lights. "Now, there's just one other thing," the woman said. "I can't start using you until you notify your counselor. That's part of our agreement with Camp Sunnyside."

"I can tell her right away," Erin said.

"The sooner you tell her, the sooner you can get to work. Hurry up, it's almost ten-thirty already. We'll meet you at the softball field."

"This is great for me," Tish said in satisfaction.

And for me, Erin thought. True, it wasn't as good as having a part in the movie, but she still had a chance at that. Getting to know the director could only increase her chances of getting hired. As soon as he found out what a great actress she really was, he'd be happy to hire her.

"I'll be right back," Erin promised. She smiled at everyone and gave them a wave, then turned and started running up to the archery range. Part of her wished she could start yelling at the top of her lungs, but she knew that wouldn't be cool at all.

The girls from cabin six were just coming off the range. Carolyn was leading them back down the hill.

"Guess what, everybody?" Erin called as she reached them. "They want me to be a stand-in." She tried to sound as casual as possible.

"You're kidding!" Katie shrieked. "Does that mean you're going to get to meet Rod Laney?"

"Probably," Erin said with a shrug. "Carolyn, I need your permission."

Carolyn nodded. "Fine with me, Erin. I'll go tell Ms. Winkle. See you back at the cabin, girls."

"What is a stand-in?" Megan wanted to know.

"Oh, it's kind of like, you take the star's place before they start shooting the movie," Erin said quickly, running the words together.

"Huh?" Megan said.

"Never mind, you wouldn't understand. It's a show-biz term."

"You mean you're going to have to be with that awful Tish all day?" Sarah asked.

"She's not so bad," Erin said.

"I didn't think she was very nice," Megan remarked.

"No kidding," Katie agreed.

"Erin, do you like her?" Trina asked.

Erin shifted from one foot to the other. "Not particularly."

"Then why do you want to be with her?" Katie challenged.

Erin rolled her eyes. "So I can get a part in the movie." The second the words were out of her mouth, Erin was sorry she'd said them.

"Then you *are* using her," Trina said.

"I am *not.*"

"Erin Chapman," Katie said, staring hard at her. "You are too using her, and you know it! You're using her the same way you used me!"

"Don't be dumb," Erin murmured.

"You used Megan, too," Sarah said hotly. "You got her scared to be an extra so that you could take her place!"

Megan's hands flew up to her cheeks as the truth hit her.

"It's not true," Erin insisted. But none of them believed her, she could tell.

"That was really rotten," Megan said, in a small voice.

Erin felt a hot blush rise up into her cheeks. What an idiot she was for telling them the truth about Tish! "So what if I'm using her?" she said.

"I'm not hurting her—and I didn't hurt you! You know something, you're all going to be really sorry you treated me this way when I'm a big star! I'll know a lot of movie stars, and I won't even introduce you! And if you say you know who I am, I'll say I never even met you! I'll be traveling all over the world, and you'll be spending your summers the way you always do—at stupid Camp Sunnyside!"

With that, Erin ran off toward the softball field before she had to listen to another word from any of them.

Chapter 8

Striding purposefully, Erin made her way to the ball field, where the shot was already being set up.

"Hi, I'm here!" she told Jane Truby, the director's assistant.

"Come with me," Jane said matter-of-factly, walking Erin out to the middle of the outfield. "There's your mark." She pointed to a chalk mark on the grass.

"Um, what am I supposed to do exactly?" she asked.

"Just stand there," Jane answered. "Herb is going for a cloudy look, and he wants to see if he can block out the sun with some screens."

How weird, Erin thought. Why didn't they just wait for the right weather? Why try to turn a sunny day into a cloudy one? Nevertheless, that's exactly what they were trying to do. The crew people were putting up a big nylon screen

93

strung up on poles. Other people were mounting huge lights behind the fabric.

Erin stood on her mark and watched. It was sort of interesting—for about two minutes, that is. After half an hour, it became *excruciating*.

Finally, the lighting men seemed to have the screens set the way they wanted them. But just when Erin thought she was going to have a chance to rest her aching legs, the lighting crew started having some kind of trouble.

"Try a 420 bulb in that," one of the older men barked. "That should do it."

But it didn't. Erin's legs were killing her now. She tried to stretch them standing in place, but that didn't work. Erin looked around. It didn't seem like anyone was paying the least bit of attention to her, so she stepped off her mark and shook out her legs.

"What's with the stand-in?" one of the crew called to Jane Truby.

Erin felt her cheeks burn. If he had a complaint, he could have come to her about it, couldn't he? She scooted back to her mark. "That's better," the man said, addressing her directly this time.

The sun came out from behind a cloud, and Erin felt hot. Real hot. How long had she been standing there, anyway? It felt like *years*.

"It's a scorcher today, huh?" one of the lighting men complained to another.

"I'll say," the other one agreed.

Beads of sweat started trickling down Erin's forehead. Darn! Why hadn't she worn a hat?

Erin noticed most of the crew had cold drinks. But no one bothered to offer her any.

"I think we got it," the first lighting man said, after what seemed like an eternity. Though she was exhausted from doing nothing, Erin managed to smile weakly. Herb Ritter was looking at her intently through the camera lens.

Maybe he was finally noticing her! Maybe the camera was helping him see that she had star quality. Erin crossed her fingers behind her back. Was this going to be her big moment?

"There's a shadow on her hair," Herb said, ignoring Erin completely.

Erin's spirits sagged. He hadn't been thinking about her at all. He only cared about his stupid lights and shadows!

"It's that tree, Herb," said the lighting man. "If you want to lose the shadow, you've got to lose the tree, or wait for the sun to move."

"We'll just have to wait then," Herb said with a shrug. "But keep working on it anyway. Maybe we can backlight her for a halo effect."

What was he talking about? Did she have to keep standing there? Erin felt like screaming inside. When were they going to make the stupid movie, anyway?

Then Jane Truby blew her whistle. "Thirty, everybody!" she called out.

"Take a break, kid. Lunch is here," the lighting man told Erin. Surprised that something good was finally happening, Erin smiled with relief. She shook out her left leg. It was numb.

"Okay, everybody. Wolf down a little lunch, and we'll see you back here in half an hour," Herb told everyone.

Several yards behind the camera, Jane stood holding a couple of huge brown paper bags. "Who gets Swiss and tomato?" she called out as the hungry crew walked over to her.

"I'm famished," Erin told the lighting man as she walked toward Jane.

"Crew first, crew first," he said, elbowing her aside and rushing toward the food.

How rude!

"Erin, hi!" Tish called, walking up from behind her.

Erin's face brightened. "Hi, where were you all morning?"

"In the trailer, relaxing. It's too hot to be out here, that's for sure," the actress said. "How's it going?" She didn't sound very interested in finding out.

Erin gulped. What could she say? Her experience this morning had definitely been less than thrilling. In fact, it had been *horrible*. But then, "no pain, no gain," as they said at her exercise class back home. All this agony would be worth it when she got to be in the movie.

"I'm having a great time!" Erin lied.

"Yuck. I don't know how you can say that," Tish said. "Anyhow, I'm glad it's you out there, not me. I'd be melting away by now."

Erin bit her tongue. She *was* melting, but there was no way she was going to let Tish know that. Oh well, at least now, she could eat something, and get a cold drink.

The two girls walked over to Jane. "What did you order, Tish?" the assistant director asked.

"Shrimp salad and iced mint tea," the actress answered.

"Here you go." Jane handed Tish her lunch and looked at Erin. "What do you get?"

Erin was confused. "Nobody asked me to order."

"Sorry, we must have forgotten," Jane said. But Erin couldn't help feeling she didn't look that sorry.

"There's a tuna salad sandwich that no one has claimed. Do you want that?"

Hungry as she was, there was no way Erin was going to eat tuna. To her, it had to be the grossest food ever created.

"No, thanks," Erin mumbled.

"I'd give you half of my sandwich, but I'm really starved," Tish said. "Come on, let's go sit on that bench. It's nice and shady."

Erin followed Tish to the bench and they sat down. Erin watched as the actress unrolled an enormous shrimp salad sandwich. Shrimp salad happened to be Erin's favorite.

"What scenes are we doing the rest of the day?" Erin asked, trying to ignore the hunger pangs in her stomach and the sight of Tish stuffing her face and drinking her iced tea.

"Well, there's the ball field scene. I catch a ball and win the game. And after that, there's the lake scene with Rod. We're walking past the lake, and he pushes me in, you know, as a joke. Ha. Funny joke. Like I'm really looking forward to getting drenched, you know?"

Tish slurped her iced tea and took a huge bite of her sandwich, while Erin sat there, dying for a sip of something cold, or the smallest bite of food. No wonder Tish didn't have any friends, Erin thought. She was incredibly selfish!

Soon Jane blew her whistle, and lunch was over. The crew disposed of their lunch bags and got back to their positions. Erin dragged herself over to the mark she'd been standing on all morning.

"Listen up," Herb shouted. "We're going to shoot this one now."

A thin boy wearing a plain red tee shirt stepped in front of the camera lens with a black-and-white clap board. "*Camp Capers,* scene thirty-eight, ball field," he said, snapping the clapper. Erin held her breath, waiting. This was the moment when she was going to actually get to see them make a movie.

"Quiet please," Herb called. Erin stood stock still, like everyone else. She was startled when Herb yelled at the top of his lungs, "Get that stand-in out of there! She doesn't belong in the shot, you idiots!"

Herb was really mad. Erin was paralyzed with fear for a minute. Suddenly she understood what Tish had been complaining about.

A big hand yanked at Erin's arm. "You heard him! Get out!" the lighting man said, not very nicely.

Erin passed Tish, who was walking toward the mark. Tish ignored her.

"Okay, action!" Herb shouted as soon as Tish got into position. "Ready, Tish?"

One of the crew gently tossed a softball at Tish, who caught it. "Look happy," Herb called out to Tish. "You just won the game, remember?"

"Camp Capers, scene thirty-eight, take two," the boy with the clap board said again, snapping the top down.

The crew member tossed another ball. This time Tish missed it. "Okay, let's have it again," Herb said.

"Camp Capers, scene thirty-eight, take three."

Tish caught another ball. And another and another and another, as they shot take after take. Tish dropped more balls than she caught. Watching her, Erin couldn't help thinking: And I thought *I* was bad at softball!

After take twenty-seven, Herb decided the grass wasn't green enough, so a few crew members were ordered to spray the grass with green paint. And Erin had to stand on her mark, breathing the noxious fumes while they did.

The whole thing took so long that they had to forget about shooting the scene by the lake and put it off till tomorrow. Erin couldn't believe it. All that whole long afternoon, they'd shot only about ten seconds of film! Still, by the time Herb called a halt for the day, Erin felt like cheering. At last, her long, boring ordeal was over.

Oh, well, Erin consoled herself. So what if nothing good happened today? Maybe tomorrow would be better. Who could say what would happen? Hey—she might even catch a break, and actually wind up being in the movie!

She cheered herself by trying to think of how she'd glorify her day when she described it to her cabin mates. But she was so tired and hungry she could barely think.

It didn't matter. They probably weren't speaking to her anyway.

Chapter 9

The next day, when Erin got to the movie set down by the lake, Jane waved her over. "I have good news," she said. "You're going to be working with Rod Laney on today's shoot."

Well, that could be interesting, Erin thought. She smiled and nodded.

Jane explained the set-up of the shot. Rod, who was playing a camp counselor, and Tish, playing a spoiled camper, would walk along the lakefront and out to the end of the swim dock. Herb Ritter hoped that this scene would be one of the funniest scenes in *The Camp Capers*.

"Rod doesn't use a stand-in, so you'll get to rehearse with the man himself," Jane said. "Let me show you where your starting mark is."

Jane took her to her mark, and pointed out her destination at the end of the pier. Erin tried to listen, but in her mind she was planning how she'd tell her friends back home about working with Rod Laney. That alone would turn her into a celebrity.

". . . the staff assured us you were a good swimmer," Jane was saying, but Erin barely heard her.

Just then, a young man with knobby knees and glasses walked up behind Jane. He had a khaki hat pulled down over his forehead. He looked vaguely familiar to Erin, but she couldn't quite place him.

"Jane," he said, "is there another marker on the pier?"

Erin glanced off toward Herb Ritter and the cameraman. Somewhere, very near by, was Rod Laney, and soon she was going to actually meet him—in person! Erin squinted into the sun, searching for the movie star.

"Hi," the guy with the knobby knees said.

Erin just nodded in return and kept on looking for Rod Laney.

"Listen up, everyone," Herb was yelling. "Let's try a couple of rehearsals."

The knobby-kneed guy was standing next to Erin now. She shot him an annoyed look. If he didn't leave soon, he was going to get in Rod Laney's way.

"Action!" Suddenly, the guy was walking with her. Erin turned her face up to his and realized that under those glasses were the greenest eyes the movie world had ever known.

102

And when he smiled, a glorious crooked smile, she knew without doubt. She was standing right next to Rod Laney.

"Are you a camper here at Sunnyside?" he asked.

Erin couldn't believe it. He wasn't really that good-looking in person. Oh, he was okay, but certainly not the Adonis he'd always seemed to be. Just a regular, good-looking guy.

"Yes, I am," she answered.

But that was all they ever got to say to each other, because every second they were together, the director or the lighting men was barking some order or other.

After about a million walks down the lake-front to the pier, Erin's legs were beginning to ache. After a while, Rod went to change into his costume, while Erin had to walk alone twenty or so more times. What a bore!

"Get the stand-in out of there!" Herb shouted. Erin heaved a sigh. She might as well have been made of plastic for all the movie director cared.

"Tish!" Jane yelled, walking toward the trailer that was brought to every different location.

Looking lovely, Tish stepped out of the trailer and went to her mark. She and Rod began their walk as the cameras rolled. Erin watched them do dozens of takes, and to her, each one looked exactly like the others.

Erin found herself thinking about Katie and Trina and the other girls of cabin six. They were somewhere on the camp grounds, riding horses, or playing tennis, or swimming at the pool. For once, she wouldn't have minded being with them.

Hours went by. Take after take of the same old thing. Erin was considering asking Jane if she really had to stay any longer, since no one seemed to need her.

But when Tish and Rod reached the end of the pier, suddenly everyone was calling for Erin. "Erin!" Jane yelled.

"Get the stand-in right away!" Herb Ritter shouted.

Erin made her way out to the end of the pier. All eyes were on her for a change. She tossed a thousand-watt smile to the director, giving him another chance to see her as an actress instead of a statue.

When she got to the end of the pier, the lighting man called to the director. "We have the lights all worked out. This is a two shot."

Erin didn't know what that meant, but she hoped it meant she would soon be finished for the day. For that, she would be truly grateful.

"Let's rehearse this one, Rod," Herb called to him.

Oh no, thought Erin. Another million rehearsals.

"Are you ready?" Rod asked Erin. Erin wasn't sure what he meant, but she nodded yes. For a moment, she felt like an actual star. She was there, alone in front of a movie camera with Rod Laney. True, the camera wasn't rolling, but it was still there.

And suddenly, Rod put his palm out and knocked her over into the water!

"Good, Rod," Herb called, as Erin came up for air. "We wanted that unexpected quality! Very nice!"

Sputtering and bobbing in the water, Erin listened to the laughter of the cast and crew. Gritting her teeth in frustration, she realized she must have looked incredibly funny floundering around in the water. She swam to the edge of the pier and was helped up by one of the lighting men.

"Let's take that again," Herb shouted. Wildly, Erin wished for a hole to appear in the earth that she could sink into.

The rest of the afternoon was more of the same. Erin got tossed into the lake a good fifteen times, and the rest of the time she stood around waiting to get tossed. And Tish was just as dreary and obnoxious as she'd been the day before.

The shoot lasted past dinner. When it was finally over, Erin raced back to the cabin. She was actually looking forward to a relaxing evening with her cabin mates. But when she arrived, the girls seemed to be getting ready to go somewhere.

At least Trina was still speaking to her. "How'd it go today?"

"Great!" Erin lied. "I got to work with Rod Laney."

She could see Katie was dying to ask a zillion questions. But Katie was always the last to forgive. "That's nice," was all she said.

"Where are you all going?" Erin asked.

"To Pine Ridge," Trina answered.

"To see a movie," Megan added.

"Oh," said Erin. Usually, one of them would have invited her to go with them. They always included each other in whatever they did together. But now, they were avoiding looking at her.

"We're going with the cabin five girls," Sarah explained.

"Oh," Erin said, trying to act as if it didn't bother her at all that she wasn't invited.

Soon Katie had opened the door and they were all filing out. "Well, see you," Trina said. At least she had the courtesy to look sorry.

When they were gone, the cabin felt so empty. Carolyn ran in after a moment, saying,"Oh, hi, Erin! I forgot my bag. I'm taking the girls in to Pine Ridge for a movie. Want to come?"

Erin had too much pride to even consider the

invitation. "No thanks, Carolyn," she said. "I'm kind of tired."

"Oh," said Carolyn. "I understand. Movie work is hard, huh?" When Erin didn't respond, Carolyn asked, "Erin, are you all right?"

"I'm fine," Erin said stiffly. "Go on. Have a good time." But after she left, the cabin had never felt so empty. She couldn't go on like this much longer, with her cabin mates hating her. She was going to have to make amends, with Katie first of all. Once Katie forgave her, the others would follow.

And she started to plan. . . .

Chapter 10

The next morning, Erin dragged herself to the movie location near the stables. Today, Jane told her, they would be filming Tish's big scene. For about two hours, Erin stood at the corral as the lighting men adjusted and re-adjusted the big lamps shining down on her. They were having more trouble than usual, because it seemed rainy weather was coming. Every so often a huge gray cloud would come along and change the lighting effects just when they had gotten them right.

From her position at the corral fence, Erin scanned the crowd, looking for Rod. She had a piece of paper and a pen in the pocket of her jeans.

"Break time, everyone!" Jane called. "But make it short! The weather is not cooperating today."

Erin walked over to the director's assistant. "Jane, where's Rod?" she asked.

"He's inside the stables," Jane told her. "I have a feeling he wants to stay far away from Tish this morning."

Erin could understand that. Tish had been snapping at everybody in sight all morning long. Erin hurried into the stable, her paper and pen in hand. "Rod?" she called out. "Are you in here?"

Rod stepped out from behind one of the stalls. "I was just talking to Starfire here," he said, stroking the horse's nose.

"Rod," Erin began, surprised that there was a quiver in her voice. Rod was a nice person, but that didn't mean he liked giving out autographs. Erin knew that lots of stars hated being accosted by people who stuck a pen and paper in their hands. In fact, asking for an autograph had to be one of the uncoolest things to do in the entire world.

"Yes . . . ?"

"Can I . . . can I . . ." Erin faltered. "Would you give me your autograph?" There, she'd gotten it out. "It's not for me," she quickly explained. "It's for my girlfriend, Katie. She has this—this kind of crush on you, you know? It would really mean a lot to her."

She held out the pen and paper to him. Rod smiled and took them.

"No problem," he said. "But do you think she'd rather have an autographed picture?"

"Sure!" Erin blurted out. "I mean, yeah. That would be great."

"They're in my trailer. Come on back with me."

"Okay." He's nice, Erin thought as they walked to his trailer. At least he wasn't treating her like a star-struck nuisance.

"How many girls are in your cabin?" he asked. "When I went to camp, we had these long barrack-type rows of beds."

"There are five of us," she told him. "Me, my friend Katie, Trina, Sarah, and Megan. They're all your fans, of course. But Katie has a big thing about it."

"That's great," he said with a grin. "I can use all the fans I can get."

"Rod! Rod!"

Erin looked up as Tish burst through the trailer door.

"Where have you been?" she asked him. "I really wanted you to hear my monologue."

"Sorry, Tish, I was just at the stables, and Erin came in and asked me for an autograph. I'll just get her a publicity shot and then I'll listen to your monologue."

"What's more important?" Tish snapped. "Getting some lovestruck kid an autograph or hearing my monologue?"

Rod's smile was looking forced. "Obviously, hearing your monologue is important," he said. "But giving her an autograph won't take a second."

"It's not for me, Tish," Erin explained. "My cabin mate really—"

"Oh, shut up!" Tish yelled, staring straight at Erin with daggers in her eyes. "The nerve of you! I should have known you were just using me to get close to Rod. You know, the only reason you're even here is because of me—and I'm going to do something about that right now! I'm going to go tell Herb and Jane that you're interfering with the work on this movie set! I'm going to tell them I want you out of here!"

With that, she turned on her heels and left the trailer, marching over to where the director and assistant director were sitting.

"Tish, wait!" Rod called out after her. "You're getting all bent out of shape over nothing."

"Gosh . . ." Erin murmured, flabbergasted by the size of Tish's tantrum. The girl obviously had *big problems*.

"I'll try and stop her," Rod said, hurrying after Tish.

Erin trotted behind him, but she stopped in her tracks as soon as Tish got to Herb and Jane.

"This Sunnyside kid is screwing me up!" Tish told them hotly. "I know I brought her onto the set, but it was obviously a big mistake. All she

111

was trying to do was to get close to Rod Laney. Now she's bothering him for autographs and disturbing my concentration. I want her fired right now!"

Herb looked mildly annoyed. He waved one hand, like a king shooing away a fly. "She's fired. There. Do you feel better?" he asked Tish.

Erin's cheeks were burning hot. What nerve!

"This is stupid," Rod said as Jane walked over to Erin with a regretful, but not too regretful, look on her face.

"Sorry, Erin," she said. "You heard what the boss said."

"Come on, Jane," Rod said, trying to smooth things over. "Maybe after they shoot Tish's scene, she'll calm down and forget about the whole thing."

"I'm not willing to take that chance."

"No big deal," Erin said. "I'll just leave." It dawned on her that she didn't feel badly at *all* about being fired. In fact, she felt downright *relieved.*

It was all she could do to walk away, not run. Halfway back to the cabin, she realized she hadn't got Rod's autographed picture for Katie.

Oh, well, at least she'd tried. Anyway, Erin reflected, whatever else she had learned, one thing was clear—she might be the greatest actress in world history, but show business just wasn't for her.

112

Chapter 11

By the time Erin reached the stoop of cabin six, the rain had started coming down. She'd just missed it. Glad to be someplace warm and dry, she opened the cabin door.

"I'll buy Marvin Gardens and put one hotel on Atlantic Avenue," Sarah was saying.

"Oh, no," Megan moaned. "Now she has all the yellows *and* four hotels!"

The girls were huddled around a Monopoly set that was spread out on a clear area of the floor.

"Hi, everyone," Erin said.

The others barely glanced up at her, and Erin realized that she was still getting a heavy dose of the silent treatment. No wonder, thought Erin, after the crummy way she'd treated them.

"Excuse me," she said levelly. "I know you're mad, but can I talk to you guys for a minute?"

Trina looked up, then Sarah and Megan. But

Katie stubbornly kept her eyes riveted on the game board.

"Guys," Erin began, letting out a huge sigh. This time, she was going to put all pride aside. "I'm really sorry about the way I've been acting. I guess I just wanted to be in that movie so badly, I kind of forgot all about everyone else."

The other girls exchanged surprised looks. Even Trina looked as if she didn't know what to say.

"So I'm really sorry if I hurt your feelings," Erin went on. "If I did, I hope you'll all forgive me." They'd better, she thought. She couldn't go on being this humble forever.

Her words got to Trina and Sarah. They stood up and walked over to her. "Thanks, Erin," Trina said. "I forgive you."

"Me, too," added Sarah.

"And me, too," Megan said, looking up from the game board.

Erin looked down at Katie. From the way she stuck out her jaw and clenched her teeth, it was clear Katie wasn't ready to forgive at all. "How's your friend Tish?" she asked.

"She's not my friend anymore," Erin said. "In fact, she got me fired from the movie."

Everyone gasped when they heard that. "It's okay," Erin told them. "I was tired of it anyway." The next words were hard to say. "And I missed you guys."

114

There was a long silence. "You said some pretty mean things," Katie reminded her.

"I know," Erin admitted. "Like I said, I'm really sorry."

Katie bit her lip. "Well, I—"

Whatever Katie was about to say never got said, because suddenly there was a knock on the door.

"That must be Carolyn," Sarah said.

"But why would she knock?" Megan wondered.

Megan was closest to the door, so she opened it. And then she screamed. "Rod Laney!"

There was a dead silence. And then, as Rod Laney walked into the cabin, the room erupted in squeals.

Carolyn was right behind him. "I found this guy wandering in the rain, looking for cabin six," Carolyn said, grinning.

Rod was holding a manila envelope under his arm, and he wore the shy crooked grin that was his trademark. "Hi," he said. "Erin, we had to cancel the shoot because of the rain, so I thought I'd bring what you asked for. Which one of you is Katie?"

Katie rose to her feet with a dazed expression. She walked over to the man of her dreams and held out a trembling hand. "I'm Katie," she said, barely breathing. When he took her hand to shake it, Katie looked like she could pass out from sheer joy.

"Erin was telling me all about you," Rod said. "You sounded like a really neat person, and I wanted to make sure you got this." He pulled a photo out of the envelope. Swallowing hard, Katie took it, and read the inscription aloud.

" 'To Katie, one of my most special fans. Love, Rod.' Wow!" She clutched it to her chest. "Thanks."

"I've got one for each of you," Rod said. The next few moments were taken up with Rod signing each picture. Trina was blushing, Megan was giggling, and Sarah just looked blissful.

"Carolyn, could you take a picture of all of us with Rod?" Katie asked.

"If it's okay with Rod," she replied.

"Fine with me," Rod said.

Carolyn went into her room for her camera and returned quickly. They all got into position, with Sarah, Megan, and Trina crouched down in front, Katie on one side of Rod, and Erin on the other.

"Okay, everybody," said Carolyn, raising her camera to her eye. "Smile!" It was a totally unnecessary comment.

When she was finished, Rod turned to Katie. "You've got a good friend here," he said, nodding toward Erin.

116

Katie suddenly became very interested in her sneakers. "Yeah."

"I'd better get back to the trailer and study my lines. It's been great meeting you all." A chorus of "thank you's" followed Rod to the door.

"I'll show you a shortcut back," Carolyn said, following him out.

When the door closed, Katie gazed at the picture she was clutching tightly. "I can't believe this just happened."

"And you owe it all to Erin," Trina reminded her.

"I know." Katie turned to Erin and actually smiled.

"Erin," Sarah said suddenly, "did you get fired because you asked for a picture?"

"Sort of."

"Wow," Katie said. "You really *are* a friend. I'm sorry you got fired."

Erin shrugged. "I guess I wasn't cut out to be a movie star."

"Well, if it's any consolation," Katie said, "you're a Sunnyside star. Or at least, a cabin six star."

Erin nodded. "I guess that's good enough." She tossed her head and grinned. "For now."

MEET THE GIRLS FROM CABIN SIX IN

CAMP SUNNYSIDE FRIENDS

(#10) ERIN AND THE MOVIE STAR 78181-5 ($2.95 US/$3.50 Can)

(#9) THE NEW-AND-IMPROVED SARAH
76180-7 ($2.95 US/$3.50 Can)

(#8) TOO MANY COUNSELORS 75913-6 ($2.95 US/$3.50 Can)

(#7) A WITCH IN CABIN SIX 75912-8 ($2.95 US/$3.50 Can)

(#6) KATIE STEALS THE SHOW 75910-1 ($2.95 US/$3.50 Can)

(#5) LOOKING FOR TROUBLE 75909-8 ($2.95 US/$3.50 Can)

(#4) NEW GIRL IN CABIN SIX 75703-6 ($2.95 US/$3.50 Can)

(#3) COLOR WAR! 75702-8 ($2.50 US/$2.95 Can)

(#2) CABIN SIX PLAYS CUPID 75701-X ($2.50 US/$2.95 Can)

(#1) NO BOYS ALLOWED! 75700-1 ($2.50 US/$2.95 Can)

MY CAMP MEMORY BOOK 76081-9 ($5.95 US/$7.95 Can)

CAMP SUNNYSIDE FRIENDS SPECIAL:
CHRISTMAS REUNION 76270-6 ($2.95 US/$3.50 Can)